What people are saying about

The Book of Thunder and Lightning

...you've made the slow surfacing of china-pale bodies in Dorito-coloured dirt genuinely, atmospherically spooky. More! More!
Francis Spufford

Seb Duncan's writing is fluid, vividly descriptive and is perfect for a young adult reader. We see London from the witty Victorian eyes of Tom, a ghost from 1888, who finds himself in an unlikely pairing; a hack journalist and English tutor called Simon.
Isabel Judd and Louis Chapman, editorial team at GoldDust

Seb Duncan captures the thrill of the bright lights of Piccadilly Circus and the awe that part of London has sparked for generations of visitors.
Midge Gillies, author of *Piccadilly: The Circus at the Heart of London*, *The Barbed-Wire University* and *Amy Johnson: Queen of the Air*

T0284379

The Book of Thunder and Lightning

A Novel

The Book of Thunder and Lightning

A Novel

Seb Duncan

ROUNDFIRE
BOOKS

London, UK
Washington, DC, USA

CollectiveInk

First published by Roundfire Books, 2024
Roundfire Books is an imprint of Collective Ink Ltd.,
Unit 11, Shepperton House, 89 Shepperton Road, London, N1 3DF
office@collectiveink.com
www.collectiveink.com
www.roundfire-books.com

For distributor details and how to order please visit the 'Ordering' section on our website.

ISBN: 978 1 80341 677 9
978 1 80341 678 6 (ebook)
Library of Congress Control Number: 2023946222

A CIP catalogue record for this book is available from the British Library.

Design: Lapiz Digital Services

UK: Printed and bound by CPI Group (UK) Ltd, Croydon, CR0 4YY
Printed in North America by CPI GPS partners

We operate a distinctive and ethical publishing philosophy in
all areas of our business, from our global network of authors to
production and worldwide distribution.

Any sufficiently advanced technology
is indistinguishable from magic.
Arthur C Clarke

Arnold Circus

In 1889 the demolition teams came.

They levelled the Old Nichol, only leaving fragments of the past behind Boundary Passage, Old Nichol Street, Chance Street. Some others.

By 1900, the Boundary Estate was built.

Tall, orange-bricked flats sprang up, with shared stairwells and large windows that let in the light from wide tree-lined avenues.

A round central park, Arnold Circus, was built in the estate's centre.

It was constructed on a six-foot mound using thousands of bricks from the old torn down houses.

For some reason, the architect had insisted that precisely six trees be planted in a circle.

They remain there to this day.

Glowing veins of electrons carve through ionised channels.

A negative charge travels down to the ground at great speed, its positively charged twin reaching up to meet it. The sky cracks apart like the lines on a vertical ice pond, as if opening a void between this world and the next.

Mr Tipps's Bookshop 1888

The so-called school Tom Baxter attended only taught Christian virtues, manners and the like. Tom preferred the books in Mr Tipps's bookstore on Shoreditch High Street. Bernard Tipps was a kind man and let him read as many books as he wanted for as long as he wanted.

Each day Tom would enter the shop and Tipps would slowly look up from his own reading and simply ignore him, even though he knew the boy would never buy anything. Although their relationship was not what one would call close, there was a silent understanding between them, that if Tom didn't clip anything or cause any damage, he would let him stay all day if he wanted.

The smell of the shop had become comforting to Tom; brewing tea, mingled with musty paper, with the faint whiff of Mr Tipps's black and white cat who was always sleeping in the heat of the window in the summer, or by the fire in winter. The air always seemed to be dusty. If the light from the picture window was just right, you could see tiny specks of dust spinning and bouncing into each other like mini galaxies of skin, hair and paper. As a result, Mr Tipps was forever dusting the shop and had a cloth for such work hanging out of his brown suit pocket at all times.

All the books interested Tom, even though he didn't really understand all of them and Mr Tipps sometimes read to him if he asked. Some of the stories were very strange indeed. One called Jane Eyre, about a woman kept in a cupboard or something, was one of the oddest. Mr. Dickens's Bleak House was exactly *that* in his view. Why were all these rich people, with such a lovely big house, so sad all the time?

On a day like any other, he was sleeping by the back of the shop when he noticed Tipps's cat clawing at something underneath one of the dark wood bookshelves. Hoping to find a discarded biscuit, Tom removed his cap, laid flat on his stomach and wriggled underneath the bookshelf to see what the cat was scratching at.

Reaching as far as he could into the darkness, he pulled at something heavy with his fingernails and dragged it out. It wasn't a giant biscuit but a book, a very large book. Maroon in colour with gold writing and curly leaf patterns framing the title, it was one of the most beautiful things he had ever seen. The shiny printing seemed to be indented into the cover itself. Tom's mouth moved as he read the words carefully, his fingers slowly touching the letters as he read along the title.

It was called *Thunder and Lightning* by Wilfred de Fonvielle. It was a curious book about history and electricity and had pictures of different lightning.

Tom had no idea if this was a science book, history book or indeed a book of stories. He didn't really care, because he immediately knew he loved it.

Tom showed Mr Tipps the book and hopped up to his big desk. Tom sat still as Mr Tipps read. The book began with the travels of a famous physicist and explorer.

— The Pyramids —

In the year 1805, esteemed physicist Herr Werner Siemens was confronted with a roaring thunderstorm as he investigated the high point of the pyramid of Giseh. As he raised his hand to the heavens, he witnessed flowing electrical matter escaping from his fingers. The electricity hissed as it travelled down to him and his guides stared at the terrifying sight. To their astonishment, he could direct the electricity this way and that by using a gourd with a metallic button, as if fully in control of the strange, heavenly liquid.

The illustration that sat opposite the story was of a dark stormy sky from which small electric sparks descended, as Siemens' finely robed guides raised their hands while they stood high up on the very top of the pyramid. More pointed structures could be seen scattered across the desert landscape. Tom knew about the new electricity but could lightning be controlled in such a way, could it be tamed?

'Mr Tipps, what's a gourd?'

'It's a type of vegetable, Tom, like a pumpkin,' Mr Tipps answered, without looking up from the book.

'So, you can control lightnin' with a vegetable?'

The First Storm

The following day back home at number nine Old Nichol Street, stubborn black clouds stood above like sheets of solid soot.

Anne Baxter was hurriedly taking in various items of washing from the complex tangle of lines that filled the entire area of the small, shared space.

'What *ever* are you doing, Thomas Baxter?'

Tom was holding an old potato up to the sky, squinting at it as he pulled focus between the distant lightning above and the root vegetable in his hand.

'It's Herr Werner Siemens, Mum, he managed to control lightnin'.'

'Her what?'

Tom held his other hand up to his mother, in a plea for silence. He waited. Nothing happened. Realising the error of his ways, he went running out of the open doorway towards the Roper's house as the thunder rumbled. His little legs carried him down the narrow, cobbled street. His mother ran after him. Old Joe, the drunk, was singing to himself as he smoothed his hair down, looking at his own reflection in one of the few unbroken windows as a looking glass.

He came to a halt at the Roper's. Dorris the donkey poked her head out of the windowless ground floor opening. Tom climbed up on their wall, then carefully reached over to the rooftop and dangled each leg on either side, crawling like a worm higher and higher. The rain was beginning to pelt down in big dollops, making high and low noises, hitting lead and slate.

Then, the lightning came. Bright white flashes lit the black landscape above, the air became darker, in contrast to its sudden brightness. Tom climbed to the top of the roof and pulled out his potato. Holding it up, he could see forked lightning dancing in the distance and he slowly waved the vegetable from side to side trying to make contact with it. Tom shouted to himself the words he remembered from his book.

'Although a potato is not, in and of itself, an energy source. What the potato does is to help con-duct elec-tricity by acting as what's called a salt bridge between the lightnin', allowing the elec-tron current to move freely from it to my hand...'

'Tom, what the bloomin' hell you talking about, you'll fall off that roof if you're not careful,' his mum shouted up to him.

He saw one lightning fork move towards his potato and stretched further, higher. Another flash of sheet lightning exploded above Tom's head. Then the crack of thunder seemed to split the sky in two. Tom's feet slipped on the roof; a tile fell to the ground smashing into pieces on the pavement below. Now Old Joe and his mum were shouting up to him and the rain came down sideways. The forked lightning seemed to be getting closer to the rooftop as Tom stretched higher and another clap of thunder smashed around his ears. Dorris was now screaming and banging her hooves on top of the straw filled room.

Then the rumbles came again but this time quieter. Slowly the lightning simply became grey smudges on the dark clouds stretching across the sky.

Tom, his soaked clothes weighing him down, shrugged his shoulders and lowered his potato and looked at it. He turned it this way and that, looking at it from every angle, the way someone might observe a faulty piece of mechanical equipment. He gave it a quick shake, held it to his ear and then carefully placed it back into his pocket. The first lightning experiment hadn't exactly gone to plan but at least it was a start.

He carefully reversed down the edge of the roof and jumped down to the pavement with a splash. As the last drops of rain squeezed themselves out of the sky, he looked up one last time and passed the potato to his mum.

'Thank you, Tom, that's quite enough of that. Now get yourself inside and lay the table for dinner.'

Everything was as it always was. One room containing a dark wood table to eat from. A stove in the corner. The ceiling was sagging, with the same far corner damp and bubbling like a piece of burnt butter.

Dinner consisted of a piece of dried bread each, two potatoes and a sort of gravy. The meal usually started with Tom's dad saying a prayer and ended with him sitting, beer cup in hand, mumbling to himself.

There had to be another way. Just had to. Tom was determined to find out what that other way was and he started the following morning.

Hush

Dark blue door. Filthy windows. Doormats stacked up next to brass lamps and coal buckets. Everyone knew Hush's Haberdashers in the Old Nichol.

Tom entered the shop and Theodore Hush appeared from a tiny opening in the wall of goods piled high and wide on the counter. He had a thin, mean face.

The shop always smelt of damp wood mixed with paraffin. Hundreds of mouse traps hung from the low ceiling and shiny white moth balls spilled out of glass jars like dead eyes.

Tom walked towards the counter, scrunched hat in hand.

'Yes, young man, what can I do for you?' Hush asked.

'Lookin' for work, sir,' Tom replied.

Hush looked down, eating an apple as he talked. He swallowed every last morsel, including the core, pips and all. His eyes narrowed. Assessing the potential.

'Come 'ere, lad.'

Tom edged closer to the counter.

'You're Frank Baxter's son from Old Nichol Street,' Hush said.

'Yes, sir.'

More looking. More assessing.

'How old are you now, son?'

'Thirteen, sir.'

'Bad luck about your dad losing his job as the coachman. He's too young to have his sight go like that.'

'It was only one eye, sir.'

It was only one eye sir, Hush repeated in a high-pitched voice.

'You're alright, lad. I'm only joking with you. Now *today* you might be in luck. We've got some old rolls at the back that might need a home to go to. Coffee?'

'Thank you, you're so kind, sir.'

Hush's face disappeared and Tom could hear the muffled noise of cupboards opening and closing and cups and saucers clinking from behind the wares. As he waited, he looked around the gloomy shop and wondered how Mr Hush could ever find anything when customers wanted to buy something, and how he was able to make any money from such things — bits and pieces this and that. People just needed them, he thought. Everyday things were needed every day, he supposed.

His eyes were then caught by an object that stood out. A dark blue umbrella was hung against the wall, high up, as if out of reach. Its wooden handle and shiny silk made it look out of reach of most people's pockets too.

Eventually, Hush re-entered the shop. With his stiff shuffling movements, it was as if he was always late for something or other.

'Here you go, lad, careful, it's well hot.'

He dropped a plate in front of Tom of assorted rolls surrounding a cup and saucer of steaming coffee, the aroma savoury and refreshing.

Tom launched into one of the rolls, chewing only briefly before swallowing huge hunks of bread down. As he ate, Hush couldn't help notice Tom peering over the coffee cup at the blue umbrella.

'Like it, do ya?'

'Yes, tasty. Thank you, Mr Hush.'

'Not the grub, the umbrella.' He gestured up to the wall.

'Yes, very pretty, looks pricy.'

'It's certainly that, Mr Baxter.'

'Tell me, Tom, what's your old man doing for his work now he can't drive.'

'Nothin', he's got no work. My mum's makin' and selling matchboxes now. Support Home Industries an' that.'

'Matches, eh?' Hush said, as he rubbed his bristly chin.

'Tell you what, send your mum here later, I might be able to help her out.'

'Thank you, Mr Hush, I'll tell 'er.'

With that, Tom stuffed his shirt with rolls, took one last look at the fancy umbrella and left the shop to head home. He lowered his cap over his eyes and watched shopkeepers pulling up shutters and placing items by their doors, café owners putting out tables, chairs and chalkboard menus.

As he loitered on the corner, Tom was drawn to a strange sort of music coming from across the street. It faded in and out between the carriage wheels and shop worker cries.

He followed, and came to a side road where a coach was parked by a warehouse opening. Tom walked across to look closer.

A man with a black moustache and red braces was carrying meat over his shoulder and another was lifting it up to a ledge into a big store. Smoke poured out of a small pipe in the wall, filling the street with a sweet, woody smell.

Tom edged towards the warehouse and stood looking up at the man whose brow was covered in blackened sweat. The man laughed when he spoke to the other men, he had a sort of swagger about him.

'What you up to, son?'

'Just lookin',' Tom said.

'Aint you seen meat before?'

'Not this close. No.'

'You're not 'ere to take nothing? Like one of those cosh lads, 'ere to nick me meat.' He smiled and poked Tom in his stomach. Tom just looked down at his scuffed shoes.

'I thought all you lot was in Holborn,' Tom said, looking up.

'Not now. We is *everywhere*,' he said, raising his hands in a circle.

'Even in this blood' place.'

The man continued the rhythmic carrying and lifting as they spoke.

Stretching up to the opening of the warehouse, Tom could see where the music was coming from. A boy was playing a most strange instrument. It had strings but was as tall as the boy, like a great big piece of furniture it was. The boy plucked and pulled at the fat strings. The sound soothing like water running over rocks.

'You like, no? My son gonna be famous someday.'

The man then stopped his lifting and reached inside his shirt. He pulled out a small pocket knife and held it up to Tom with wide eyes. Tom stepped back and almost fell off the curb. The man steadied him, laughing as the instrument echoed louder.

'Careful, son.'

The man clasped the knife in the palm of his hand, clicked it open with his other, and sliced off a big corner of the fatty meat and handed it over, his chest rising and falling as he laughed.

'Here you go, lad. Take that home to your mama.'

'Thank you, sir.'

He winked back at Tom, whistled to the other worker and resumed his rhythmic lifting and loading to the sound of his son's music.

Tom walked up Boundary Passage, the lump of meat and rolls under his jacket making him look like a small portly gentleman. As he walked, he hummed, making sure to avoid the deep potholes that peppered the way to his house.

Today was Wednesday — his favourite day. Each week he saved enough vegetable scraps to feed Dorris the donkey, one of the long-term residents of the Old Nichol. The Nichol had more than its fair share of wildlife. Chickens squawked and pigs snorted and the smell was something horrible. Most people had animals that brought in a little income. Chicken eggs could feed a family well, not to mention be sold in the markets or surrounding streets. Baby pigs were a good earner, even a cow had lived next door that had supplied milk to the whole street for years.

Curious that just a mile down the road there were dining rooms and brightly lit market tables covered with fresh vegetables, poultry and game. All manner of seafood was displayed on dripping ice beds, all twinkly and that, next to pies and cheeses as well as more exotic fare from faraway lands.

On cue, Dorris poked her huge head out of the broken ground-floor window with a nod and a snort. Tom hopped over the opening and stroked her hard, dusty head and reached into his pocket for the scraps, Dorris nudging his arm and tickling him as he held his nose. She limped forward on her bent front hooves.

On days like this, he liked to imagine he was a wealthy land owner. He would wake early, eat a hearty breakfast and tend to his flock before riding to market to trade in livestock, grain and vegetables. He would have a huge family of his own and people would respect him because he treated his animals so well.

As the last of the carrot tops and old cabbage were finished, the animal breathed out dryly through her nose and Tom scratched her head once more.

'Look, Dorris. I'm working on it see. I've got some plans, don't you worry. Mr Hush told me he's going to help us.' The animal bowed her head and moved in towards him.

Before setting off towards his house, he walked over to the window of the toy shop on the corner of Church Street. The picture window display contained a huge model of a house, one used for dolls and such like. On the ground floor, a model of a family ate happily at a lavish dining table brimming with roast chicken, vegetables, mini gravy dishes and wine goblets. The father sat proudly at the head of the table with a glass raised. An electric light with what looked like a thousand diamonds, hung from the ceiling above them. As Tom stared, his breath appeared on the shop window and he wiped it away to form a rectangle of clear glass that framed the scene.

He turned the corner of Chance Street.

Chance Street. Was that a joke? Someone must have had a laugh with that one.

He turned into Old Nichol Street.

Here most of the doors were missing, making the houses look like a line of startled faces, the shuttered windows the eyes, the dark open doorways the mouths. He stepped over Old Joe with his bottle and walked straight into the black mouth of number nine.

Passing along the hall and opening the left door to their rooms, he heard the screams of his baby sister, Mary. Inside, Anne Baxter gently bounced her on her knee and folded card for matchboxes. Her hands were black from the chemical paste. Her feet and lower legs were completely covered by the tiny boxes she had already made, and they spilled out across the floor of the cramped room like a fancy gown.

Frank Baxter was sitting at the table rubbing his unshaven chin and looking up to the ceiling with his one good eye at nothing in particular, an empty tankard by his side. His right eye was covered with a leather patch, his face was droopy and a small paunch had started to grow above his belt line.

'Where you been, son?'

'Went to get bread at Hush's.'

Tom flicked out his undershirt and proudly spread the meat and rolls on the table. His father grabbed a piece of bread and swallowed in one go, then handed another to Tom's mother. She nibbled at it the way a mouse nibbles cheese. Baby Mary tried to grab at her mum's bread with her podgy hands.

'Well done, lad. Put the meat by the window,' Frank said, with a full mouth.

'Mr Hush told me that he might have some work for Mum,' Tom said.

'What do you mean, *work*. What kind of work?'

'I told him about the matches and he sounded interested.'

'Everyone this side of Shoreditch is making bleedin' matches, what would he want with 'em?'

'I'm just tellin' you what he said, is all.'

'You just be careful of old Hush, son, he's not what he seems.'

'What do you mean, Dad?'

'Just keep your wits about you is all. I've heard things about him.'

'Yes, Dad.'

At that point, they heard a voice come from the street. A familiar voice. An unwanted voice. The house-jobber was here to collect rent.

A pompous man, far too well well-dressed for his age with his shirt tails hanging out, entered the hallway of number nine and knocked heavily on the door of the Baxter's lodgings. He looked behind him, confused by the missing door onto the street that he was sure had been there on previous visits and surveyed his notepad, casting his tiny pencil down the list.

'The Baxters, number nine. You're behind on rent, so that's two weeks you owe,' he said with a squeaky voice.

Anne Baxter turned to hand Mary to Frank, who was now asleep, and then twisted in the opposite direction to carefully pass the baby to Tom instead. She reached behind an empty bottle of Godfrey's cordial on the fireplace and took out the money. The house-jobber snatched it, gave out a foul smelling belch as he counted, and placed it in his leather pouch.

'Much obliged. Until next time. You really should get a door on that; you'll catch a death of cold.'

'Used it for firewood,' Tom replied.

'Righto,' the house-jobber answered, as he skipped out of the doorway looking down on his list, accompanied by his cosh-carrying bodyguard.

The Meeting at the Crown

As Theodore Hush and Arthur Snipe approached the green tiled entrance to the Crown on Redchurch Street, Hush bowed and ushered Snipe in ahead of him. Snipe could only enter if he turned sideways through the doorway. The proprietor saw who Hush was with, and immediately nodded to him to go to the back room of the pub.

They sat opposite the fireplace, the bench's wood cracking as Snipe squeezed behind the table. Inside the pub the air was greasy. The stink of the previous night's beer had seeped into the wooden floorboards and leather banquettes underneath Snipe's massive arse.

Arthur Snipe's firm presided over business from Bethnal Green up to Stoke Newington, all the way across to Islington and down to most of Kings Cross. His walking cane was by his side; it was unusual in design in that it had a silver seam running down its entire length. Made in Paris to Snipe's exacting specifications, the solid silver handle was in the shape of a woman's face, her hair flowing sideways. He called it 'Lady'. It had come in useful for certain situations pertaining to his line of work and was a reminder to all around him, that regardless of its high cost, no one would ever be able to take it from him.

On the pub's back wall, a bent looking glass framed the two men's distorted profiles. The fireplace underneath their reflection glowed red.

Snipe looked at Hush, assessing, weighing up the potential. To Arthur Snipe, the only people of interest were either partner or prey, everyone else was just a civilian. Hush was unique in that he was both partner *and* prey, and this relationship was clear to both of them.

As their beer arrived, Hush gestured for Snipe to drink before he did. Snipe took a long mouthful and wiped his mouth with the back of his hand. His red, veiny cheeks were sweaty under the dirt and the pores on his nose were open and crusty like the holes in an old dart board.

'So, Hush. All things going to plan with our little recruitment drive?'

'Perfectly, Mr Snipe. The boy is coming along nicely. I've even started to involve the mother.'

'Why, you sly old devil, Hush. Please elaborate.'

Theodore Hush beamed with pride.

'It seems she is involved in matchbox making like every other wretched family, and this is now their only means to eat and survive. I thought it a good idea to purchase a token amount for the shop, at a heavily discounted rate of course, in order to further strengthen the working *relationship*.'

'It certainly won't do any harm,' Snipe added.

'Indeed, when they are both in deep then we can continue with your plan, Mr Snipe. Which brings me to why we are here.'

Hush looked over his shoulder, carefully reached inside his pocket and pulled out an object. Looking at it one more time, he slid it across to Snipe, being careful to cover it. Snipe brought it down underneath the table and turned it over in his hand, his face lighting up with golden reflections. An engraving on the reverse read,

To Arthur, All my love, Mother.

Snipe let out a bronchial laugh and slapped the table with both of his giant hands like an amused circus bear. Considering he had never even met his mother or ever experienced anything one could describe as love, this was an amusing touch.

'*That's* what I like about you, Hush. Detail.'

Theodore Hush again blushed with pride and took a small sip from his beer and sat back relieved.

'Have you a date for the theft?' Snipe asked.

'Not yet. I'm still working on the boy. But I would say as early as October.'

'And the others?'

'I've got three more in Bethnal Green and a couple in Stepney.'

'Jolly good. There can be no delay, as the legislation date approaches. We need to be ready.'

'Of course, Arthur. I mean *Snipe*. Sorry, I mean *Mr Snipe*, sir.'

Snipe's huge face suddenly became grave and he started to stare straight ahead as if looking at something just in front of his eyes. Sounds of infant screams and slamming metal doors echoed in his mind and the handle of his cane squeaked as his clammy hands gripped it. He began to rock backward and forward in his seat.

An uncomfortable silence ensued.

Snipe laughed, as if the punchline of a joke had just been delivered, then gulped down the last dregs of his pint and abruptly stood.

'Leaving so soon, sir?'

'Got to see a man about a dog.'

Letting out a long belch, he flipped Lady up into the air with his left hand and reached with his right down to Hush's.

Their eyes met.

'Just one thing.'

'Yes, Mr Snipe.'

'No mistakes this time.'

That last word was accompanied by Hush's hand being squeezed so tightly he had to stand to attention. There was a muffled crunching sound.

Again, Snipe let out a phlegmy giggle and loosened his grip.

'*Mother*! Hush you are a right one sometimes, you know that!'

Just as soon as Arthur Snipe had arrived, he had disappeared. He never seemed to sit still, or at least stay in one place, for more than ten minutes at a time. Like a shark, continuous forward motion meant continuous survival.

Hush breathed out heavily. He opened and closed his hand, then took a good long swig of his drink, the cup shaking. Finishing his pint, he peered carefully out of the window and watched Snipe walk up the street to his waiting carriage, as the driver tipped his hat and opened the door to let him in.

The ride to the canal was short. He was accompanied by two of his largest associates. The round metal frame of the empty gasometer towered over the watery landscape, its lattice girders casting snake-like shadows in the water.

As Snipe entered the forecourt at the back of the canal, a dog started to bark and strain at his chains by the front door of the office. Dismantled boats and wooden planks were everywhere, and neat piles of coal were dispersed along the side of the water. Snipe swerved away from the dog as he entered the small outer office. Harry Simpson, the foreman, immediately stood as Snipe entered the room.

'Mr Snipe, what a surprise.'

'Well, that was the idea.'

Harry Simpson's bushy eyebrows lowered as he looked at him. They raised as he began to speak again.

'Mr Snipe, if it's about the whiskey...'

Snipe cut him off with a gesture of his fingers across his mouth and walked back out of the office, making sure to keep his distance from Simpson's dog, and looked around the large area of the forecourt as he spoke.

'All this is yours am I correct?' He waved Lady around in a circle, like a circus impresario. 'The warehouse, the offices the canal-side storage.'

'Yes, Mr Snipe.'

'Well, you must be some kind of magician then.'

'How so?' Simpson's eyebrows once again lowered.

'Well, if twenty boxes of whiskey... *my* whiskey... suddenly disappear and you own all of this...'

More gesturing with Lady.

'Then how does that happen? Unless you, or someone within your employ, must be a magician. Do you see now how the connection between said magic and the dilemma I have has been made?'

Snipe raised his cane to head height and turned to ask a question of the object.

'Now. Lady doesn't like magicians. Do you, Lady?'

He pulled the silvery handle of Lady towards his ear as if the cane itself was whispering to him.

'What's that? Oh yes, I like it, that's a good one.' He whispers back to Lady.

Snipe gestured to his men to move towards Harry Simpson's dog.

'Now. Harry, is it?'

'Yes, Mr Snipe.'

'Harry, you know the way people give second chances, or three goes and you're out, that sort of thing.'

'Yes, Mr Snipe.'

His eyebrows raised again.

'Well, that's ballocks, as far as I'm concerned, too messy and hard to keep track of. I prefer a *gesture*. It's clearer. More efficient see.'

Snipe's men had held Harry Simpson's dog, who was now straining and barking loudly.

'Two things have just occurred to me, Harry. The first is, I don't like magicians, never have. And as I told you, neither does Lady.'

'I know, Mr Snipe, you see it was just that...'

'The other fucking thing I don't like is *fucking* dogs. Unless they is racing. Now we seem to have an alignment of *dislikes*, so to speak. It sometimes happens that. Two things at the same time, stars crossing, call it coincidence, what have you.'

As Snipe talked, he edged towards Simpson's dog.

'Where's my whiskey, Mr Simpson?' he said blankly.

'I was just trying to explain, the thing is we unloaded it as you said and something happened.'

'Happened? Are we back with the magician again, I hate that bloody magician.'

'I swear, I haven't taken it. I promise I'll get it, find it, please don't hurt him, please, Mr Snipe, I'm begging you. I will do anything to find your whiskey. It was some kind of mistake. There has to be some kind of expla…'

With a sudden whistling, Lady struck down on the dog's back leg. Even though Snipe could have easily killed the animal with one or two blows, he chose not to. Pain first. Then death. Always better. The dog yelped out as Snipe's two men restrained him harder.

Snipe gave another blow, this time to his spine. The sound of metal crunching on flesh and bone.

The animal tried to fight back as it jerked its head, broke free and bit down into the hand of one of Snipe's men, who started to scream.

Lady swung down once more, this time to the animal's head, the tip of the handle imbedded in the animal's eye, ending him. Now the only sound was the screaming of Snipe's man echoing across the canal, as he cradled his mutilated, bloodied hand in the other.

Harry Simpson was ashen and shaking.

Snipe retracted Lady from the dog's skull, calmly retrieved one of his red chequered handkerchiefs — they made no sense being any other colour — and proceeded to wipe it clean next to his face as he spoke.

'Now, Mr Simpson, are we clear about the situation? I would hate to have to explain it again, what with your family being so lovely and that. Two daughters, isn't it? You must be so proud.'

Snipe clicked his fingers and nodded to his man, who promptly pulled out a piece of paper and gave it to him.

As he read, a smile came over Snipe's face. 'Ten Virginia Road, Bethnal Green. You know, I had an aunt who lived in Virginia Road. Well, I never.'

'So, I know where you live, you know where I live. All nice and cosy.'

With these words he caressed Harry Simpson's hair and crouched down to speak closely into his ear. Simpson could feel his breath on his neck as Snipe spoke.

'I'm sorry about your dog, Mr Simpson,' he whispered. 'But at least it wasn't one of your daughters, eh?'

On the surface of the canal, the black reflection of the gasometer seemed to heave and shimmer in time with Arthur Snipe's deep breathing as he stood, brushed soot off his coat and gestured for his men to leave.

The Boundary Estate, August 2022

The homeless man jerked his shopping trolley one step at a time up to the park. When he reached the top, the trees enclosed him like a pair of warm hands. He sat down on one of the benches with a huff and his hat trembled as the wind whipped around him. He reached into his pocket for a fag butt, lit it and looked down at his big toe that wriggled out of one of his shredded trainers. As he gazed at the orange sparks blowing up to the starry sky, he hardly noticed the low hum coming from underneath his feet. It gently shook the loose paving slabs from underneath the bench. One popped up with a puff of red dust. Four tiny fingers and a thumb appeared from the gap, the hands white as chalk, creased and dry. The fingernails began scraping at the bench, wood chips dropping down and blowing away. The sound of children could be heard below, laughing and whispering *I don't like mutton, it's smelly, I don't like mutton, it's smelly, I don't like mutton, it's smelly.*

The Deal

The following week at Hush's invitation, Tom entered his shop. He noticed something different about the interior. Although it was full of his usual household wares, a large stack of matchboxes had been placed next to a big sign displaying the words SUPPORT HOME INDUSTRIES. LOCAL MATCHES FOR LOCAL PEOPLE. They were the same design as his mother's; with the red stripe on the cover and there must have been a hundred of them neatly piled by the countertop. Hush appeared from nowhere with his arms folded.

'Well, what do you think?'

'Looks good, Mr Hush. You bought so many.'

'Well, we all need to help each other, Tom, don't we. Now, what about some breakfast. Coffee?'

'Thank you, Mr Hush, I am so grateful.'

'Yes, you are, aren't you, Tom.'

Hush's head disappeared behind the counter in the usual way, but this time he returned into the shop faster than before.

The tray was buckling with rolls, sandwiches and a large cake of some sort, its white icing beginning to melt down over the moist flaky sponge. Tom moved his hand towards it but Hush jerked the plate just out of reach.

'Careful, lad. Let me cut you a slice.'

As he cut, he spoke.

'Yes, Master Tom, we all need to be grateful, isn't that what the Bible says?'

'Yes, sir, it does.'

As he spoke, he pointed the large knife towards the plate.

'You see this cake here? It's a bit like life.'

'What do you mean, Mr Hush?'

'Well, some slices are for me and some slices are for you, aren't they? If I give you a piece of cake, you have to give me something in return. Some people have more than others. Right?'

As he spoke, he slowly took the plate back to Tom, but before giving it to him, placed his hand on his shoulder.

'This food, this coffee. The matches. It all costs money, Tom. I've done something for you, so now you have to do something for me.'

'Like a job, Mr Hush?'

'Yes, you could call it that.'

'I'd love a job. Is it working here? Is it a job in your shop? If it's not I can do your cleanin' if you need it.'

'Slow down, lad. Slow down.'

He handed him the cake and continued to speak as Tom began to eat.

'No, this job requires a lot more skill. More *agility*. Stealth.'

'But before I tell you what it is, finish your cake, have your coffee. I want to show you something.'

'Sounds exciting, Mr Hush,' Tom answered, with his mouth full.

When Tom finished, Hush carefully took the plate from him, turned the open sign round on the glass front door, looked left and right down the street and led him to one end of the long counter where a narrow red velvet curtain hung.

Pulling it across revealed a three-foot wide recess with a dark wall at the back of it. He reached to his left under the counter and pulled a brass lever, which caused the wall to make a creaking noise as a hidden door opened inwards. Hush looked around once more and gestured for Tom to enter, and they both walked through into a dark passage that led to a broad room.

The space was lit with the amber glow of two small lamps and the elongated shadows of hanging cups looked like sleeping bats, swinging from side to side. The sink dripped like a ticking clock, the smell unfamiliar and musty.

'Now, Tom. When we help each other, we also have to keep secrets. It's like when you have competitors, you don't tell your enemy all your secrets, do you?'

'S'ppose not, Mr Hush,' Tom answered, wiping a crumb from his mouth and looking around the room with interest.

'Well, that's what *this* is like. Trade secrets. *Top* secret.'

Hush placed his bony finger over his mouth, winking.

Along the back of the wall was another red velvet curtain stretching all the way across. Hush pulled a sashed rope dangling to its side and the curtain rippled across. Tom swallowed down his last mouthful.

From the floor to the ceiling, every type of clock or pocket watch could be seen. There were modern silver carriage clocks, small gold pocket watches, giant display clocks designed for posh homes. Tiny antique clocks with gold detailing. There must have been over two hundred items on display and they chirped like a wall of golden mechanical insects.

'But I know I can trust you because *I* helped you, and *you* helped your family. Because you're the boss now. You're the *big man*. Top boy.'

Hush moved towards Tom, and Tom moved his back against the door that was no longer there.

Hush lowered his voice, almost to a whisper.

'There's a very special item I need you to acquire. It's even more valuable than any of these things here.'

'Sounds exciting. Where is it?'

'Oh, not far from here. Islington.'

'When should I get it?'

'I have it on good authority that tomorrow night the owner will be out. So, you can do it then. The house is off Essex Road, just on the corner of Halliford Road, so it's safe.'

'If the owner's out, how will I get it, Mr Hush?'

'Don't you worry about that, Tom. I'll explain.

'Above his, I mean *the* front door, there is a small ledge that gives you access to a window that will be open for you to enter. It's the indoor privy, see. Out of his, I mean *the* privy, turn right and walk along the hall, that's where you'll find the master bedroom. In there, to the right you'll see a large chest of drawers.

'Got it so far?'

'Ledge, privy, hall, chest of drawers.'

'Good lad.

'Now, inside the top right-hand drawer, you'll find a gold pocket watch. That's your clip. Leave the way you entered. That's it. Easy peasy, see.'

'What's a clip, Mr Hush?'

'It's a bit like a game. You like games don't you, Tom?'

Hush winked and handed Tom a slip of paper.

'Here's the address.'

Tom looked down at the scribbled note written in Hush's spidery writing, reading each word carefully, his tongue clicking as he read.

290 Ann-ette Cre-scent, Essex Road (on the corner of Halliford Street), London N1.

'Just one question, Mr Hush,' said Tom raising his hand as if in a classroom.

'Name it.'

'Why aren't *you* clipping the watch?'

Hush looked down at his hands and fiddled with his fingers, found an old receipt in his waistcoat pocket and pretended to read it.

'Well, Tom, I'm too big to fit in the window, aren't I? It's not for me to do this kind of work. You're far more agile, younger, see. *Smarter.*'

He tapped his head.

'But sorry, Mr Hush. I don't understand. Isn't this against the law? Why doesn't the gentleman who owns the watch just sell it to you for yer shop like all the others you've got. I'm sure you'd get a good price. What with you being so clever an' that.'

Hush was now standing right over Tom and the boy could smell his oily mutton breath on his face as he whispered to him once more.

'It's simple. If you don't clip it, there will be no more cakes and rolls and I shan't be needing any more matches from your mum, that's for sure. Is that clear, Master Tom? I've shown you my secret and now we're mates. We wouldn't want anything to happen to you, now you've seen all of this. If you tell anyone, something bad might happen to your mum or baby Mary. That wouldn't be good would it now?'

Tom thought for a few moments.

'I wouldn't tell anyone about what I saw, Mr Hush, the clocks an' that.'

'I know, Tom, but you have to prove that to me now. Prove it by doing that little job,' he said frowning, almost apologetically.

'But... I thought you wanted to help me... and to work in your... I understand now,' he said looking down to the floor and wiping his eye.

Hush also looked to the floor as he spoke.

'Now op it, I've got things to be getting on with. You can take the rest of that cake with you if you like.'

As Hush pulled the curtain across covering the clocks, the hanging bats swayed gently once more. Tom was ushered back into the shop.

Stepping out onto the pavement, he didn't even notice the noise of the streets, the shop keepers with their boards or the crowds walking by. He was almost hit by a carriage as he crossed the road and the driver swore at him. Tom headed back to his house. He ran all the way.

Home

That night when Tom returned home his mum was boiling potatoes on the stove as always, the steam rising to the ceiling and dripping down like oily raindrops. But there was also something different. A lightness Tom couldn't quite put his finger on. The room seemed more orderly. Homely.

Frank Baxter, who was playing with Tom's sister on the floor with two empty matchboxes, jumped up.

'Here he is! The man of the moment.'

Frank knocked off Tom's hat and ruffled his hair.

'What's the matter, lad, why the long face?'

'Nothin' Dad. Just been busy an' that.'

'Too right, son. You know what, that Hush isn't so bad after all. Maybe I was wrong about him.'

'Yes, Dad.'

'Now, get that table laid. Just because you're a big businessman now doesn't mean you can shirk off from the housework. We're having roasted bloater tonight, courtesy of Mr Thomas Baxter Esquire Enterprises!'

As his mother bent down to open the iron hearth, she gave him a shy smile. But it was so much more than just a smile, it showed something he had never experienced before, let alone from his mother, and it was something he would never forget. She gave Tom a wink and heaved the giant fish out of the oven, and placed it on the table as they sat down to eat.

Anne Baxter said grace. As Tom closed his eyes all he could see were thousands of gold ticking clocks chattering away and Theodore Hush's face in the low orange light. As the secret door slowly closed, the light disappeared, the prayer complete. Tom opened his eyes and to his shock his father stood with a cup of beer in his hand.

'God bless this house and the food he gives us. But more than anything, God bless Thomas Baxter!'

'Alright, Dad, that's enough, it's only some matches.'

Frank's eyes looked to his side with resentment, then promptly sat down, almost falling backwards in the process.

They began to eat in silence. Autumn air blew in through the broken window and disturbed the flame from the lamp sitting in the middle of the table. Tom looked up from his plate and watched his mother enjoying the fish as she ate with small, patient bites and resumed with his own plate of food, which he found hard to swallow.

'Dad?'

'Yes, son,' Frank replied with a full mouthful of bloater; pieces of the fish falling down on his chin.

'I need to work with Mr Hush tomorrow night. Late. Really late.'

'Oh, why's that?'

'Somethin' about a big delivery for his shop. They come at odd times and he can't do it during the day because he'd have to close up.'

'You do what you have to. You're the boss now.'

'Tom?'

'Yes, Dad.'

'I'm proud of you, mate. Really am.'

He moved his hand on to his, and squeezed it. As his eyes welled up with tears, he quickly pulled it away and to distract him, raised his cup once more.

'To Tom.'

Anne joined in.

'Tom!'

As if understanding, Mary gurgled away in the corner as she tapped a matchbox on the wooden floor.

The Clip

Over in Islington, the fog was hanging low in front of elegant terraces. The only sound was Tom's squeaky shoes as he walked along Essex Road. He came to a stop, looked behind him and down the road ahead. In the moonlight, the curve of Annette Crescent looked like a giant set of clean, white teeth in a smiling mouth. Smoke was coming from one of the chimneys at one end of the crescent, and below it, just one solitary window was lit, its soft amber hue reminding Tom of Theodore Hush's secret room. Staying on the other side of Essex Road, Tom walked carefully towards the opposite end of the crescent to number 290.

He could just make out the black opening of the window as Hush had promised. He reached up to the black painted railings to access the ledge. He noticed a movement to his left. Looking round he saw a stray dog sitting upright, staring at him. Tom looked straight into its silvery, moon reflected eye. The animal seemed to be involved in some form of communication with him. After two silent minutes, content with their wordless negotiation, the dog turned and ambled off down the road.

Tom jumped up, his scuffed shoes bending on the railings, his hands stretching up to the ledge. It was easy to reach over and then grip the window sill. For a few seconds, he dangled off the ledge then managed to pull his whole body up to stand. Tom slipped into the open window by raising it ever so slightly and swinging each leg into the slit of darkness.

He dangled both legs inside and down on top of a faint white shape he guessed was the privy itself. His legs met the seat and it rattled as he steadied himself and jumped down as quietly as he could. The stink in the small room was rotten and he placed his hands over his nose and mouth. He pushed the door outward and a dog's bark echoed in the distance. He stepped forward, his shoes sinking into a soft rug, moving to the right, trying to adjust his eyes to the pitch black interior of the hallway. He stopped and closed his eyes for a few seconds. When he opened them, he could just see a long hall with large paintings on either side. There was a dark rectangle at the end to the right that he took for the bedroom doorway. Stepping forward silently he entered and turned right to where the chest of drawers sat.

As his eyes adjusted further, they began to pick out details in the room. A four-poster bed stood to his left at the back of the room. The large floor to ceiling double windows were letting in so much moonlight that Tom was nervous that he could be seen from outside. Crouching down, he attempted to pull out the drawer above his head but it was too heavy and stiff, so he stood to get a better purchase and slowly edged it out. He placed his hand inside and could feel soft fabric, like silk or cotton. Reaching further back, he knocked on something hard and heavy. He gripped the cold, metallic object and pulled it out along the wooden surface of the drawer. The watch was huge in his hands, its shiny surface reflecting light up to the ceiling. He turned it over and he could just about read the words on the back by tilting it towards the moonlit window.

To Arthur, All my love, Mother.

Tom thought he heard a sound and stopped.

He carefully placed the watch in his inner pocket and turned to exit the door but when he tried to step through it, his body bounced back as it hit something large and solid. Then the gaslight went on.

The bulk spoke.

'What do have we here?'

Standing in front of Tom was a man who filled the entire doorway.

Tom ducked down and dived between the man's legs and ran straight down the hall from where he came. The bulk turned and gave chase. Tom ran into the stinking privy room, jumped up and reached for the window opening which was now closed.

He tried to pull the window up but it was jammed, as sweat poured down the back of his neck. He turned and ran right into the bulk again blocking the way out of the privy.

Arthur Snipe held Tom by the throat and searched his jacket, pulling out the watch with a jerk of his massive hand.

'Oh dear, oh dear. You seemed to have clipped, I mean, *stolen*, one of my most treasured items. I shall have to contact the police immediately.'

Arthur Snipe dragged Tom down the stairs and through to the front door as the boy screamed.

'It wasn't me; it was Hush, it was Hush who told me to do it.'

'Hush, who is this Hush, whatever are you talking about, son? You are going straight to the police station.'

Outside, Snipe's driver was ready to take them, and he swiftly ran to the back of the carriage and opened its door to let them in. With one hand, Snipe gripped Tom by his breeches and threw him in the back as if he was an item of luggage and followed in after him, slamming the door.

'Old Street Police Station!'

The driver jumped up and whipped the horses into action, their hooves hitting the cobbles, sending leaves and grit spinning behind them.

The Court Case

Just some weeks from that night, the large magistrates' court was packed to the rafters. On one side, behind the raised wooden panels sat the jury, opposite sat the public onlookers, eagerly chatting away before the next case to be brought forth. Tom Baxter and two other boys were led through to the dock and placed before the shackles fitted on a wooden plinth. The jailor could hardly stretch the boys' arms high enough to reach them and their little hands fitted through the manacles without the need for them to be unfastened. The Clerk, with eyes like one horizontal slit, vertical hair sprouting this way and that, combined with a neatly swept-back beard, had the appearance of a man with his head placed upside down. He sat and banged his gavel. The tittering chat piped down and the Clerk read from his notes with a yawn.

'Case number two three eight, two three nine and two forty. All three stand accused of stealing personal possessions from a private residence on July third, August ninth and October twentieth in the year 1888. Are you guilty or not guilty?'

Crouching down, the jailor whispered out of the side of his mouth to the three children.

'Say, *not guilty.*'

'Not guilty.' The children replied in unison.

The Clerk continued.

'How will you be tried?'

The jailor prompted once more.

'Say, *by God and my country.*'

'By God and my country.' The children answered.

'Unless there is no further evidence for this case, I charge all three of you to 30 days' labour and you will be taken immediately to the children's prison.'

As he raised his gavel once more, the court assistant pushed his way through the crowd with a slip of paper and spoke into the Clerk's ear. Clearly irritated by this inconvenience, the Clerk banged his gavel to quieten down the chirping crowd.

'It seems there is a development. Do we have a Mr Arthur Snipe in the court?'

'Yes, your honour.' A booming voice came from the gallery.

The members craned their necks to see.

'And so what do you have to say on this matter?'

The bench creaked as Arthur Snipe stood and cleared his throat into his red handkerchief.

'Thank you, your honour. I would first like to say that even though I am in fact the victim of all three of these crimes and that the world has indeed turned into a dangerous place, I cannot without conscience send these poor wretches to prison in this way.'

The court chattered excitedly.

'So, what do you *propose,* er, Mr...'the Clerk raised his eyeglasses to his nose and read the note again, 'Snipe?'

'Sadly, God has not bestowed upon me a wife or indeed children of my own. I would be prepared to take them in for work in my business, to set them on the right path so to speak. Your honour, I am willing turn the other cheek if the court allows.'

The gallery behind Snipe erupted into noisy chit-chat.

The gavel was banged impatiently. Silence fell upon the court once more.

The Clerk gestured to the court members and they huddled together around his large paper strewn table. After five minutes of deliberation, the Clerk turned to Arthur Snipe who stood again. He peered down at his slip of paper with his singular eye slit.

'Mr Snipe you are the owner of Snipe Paints and Chemicals, 128 Shoreditch High Street, is that right?'

'The very same.'

The Clerk continued.

'And you would be prepared to *employ* these boys, without a second thought?'

'I would indeed. If God gives us all a chance to do some good, when we...'

The gavel banged one last time and the Clerk waved his hand away to Snipe.

'The arrangement with Mr Snipe's work offer will stand. However, as the children are fortunate to have parents and caregivers of their own, they will remain in their own homes. All charges will be dropped, and this case is now closed. Make sure the boys' parents are informed and given the necessary paperwork. Next!'

In front of the court, a journalist from the Evening Standard pushed through the crowds and winked at Arthur Snipe as he stepped out of the magistrates' court.

'Mr Snipe. Is it true that you are dropping the charges against the three boys who stole from you?' he asked unnecessarily loudly.

'Yes, I couldn't live with the idea that these young unfortunates would be punished so severely for such a small crime. Even though one of the items stolen was very dear to me, I feel it was the *Christian* thing to do.'

A crowd had begun to gather to observe the exchange.

'The court report said you would be employing them in your factory. This seems extremely generous.'

'In this age, so many of us are affected by poverty, none so much the young.'

He took out his red handkerchief and started to dab at his eye as he continued.

'If I can do my bit to help these poor little urchins, I will sleep soundly in the knowledge that God is indeed with all of us. Thank you.'

Snipe winked back to the reporter and reached up to enter his waiting carriage as it twisted sideways under his weight, leaving the gathering crowd behind. The reporter scribbled his notes and he hailed a coach which took him straight to Fleet Street.

That evening the newspaper seller screamed out the latest local headlines.

'West End final! West End final! Arthur Snipe to employ burglars who robbed his house! Local politicians name Snipe as one of 1888's men of the year!'

Back Home

Back at number nine Old Nichol Street the atmosphere was thick with silence. Anne Baxter fed Mary, her leg bouncing as she looked every now and again back at Tom who was lying on his front, sobbing. His father's belt was hung over the chair and Frank was drinking the last dregs from his cup. The court paperwork sat in his lap as he spoke.

'Typical, Tom. Start something good and you 'ad to muck it up with this. Poor old Hush. He gave you a chance and *now* look at you. I should give you more of a hidin' later when your bum 'eals over. Now get this tidied up and when you done it get out. I don't want to see the sight of you for a few hours.'

'It's not simple, Dad. I was trying to help. Help you and Mum. He forced me. It wasn't even a job. He forced me, Dad, I couldn't tell you.'

'Excuses, excuses. Now you'll learn what work is. The paint place is real work. Hard work. You'll be getting tuppence for it an' all.'

'Least *I* got a job out of it.'

Frank raised his hand.

'Frank, enough,' Anne shouted as she held his raised fist back.

Frank strained for a few moments and then lowered his arm before flicking his eye at Tom in the direction of the pantry area.

Tom limped over to the sink and started to wash the plates and pans. In the watery reflections he could see his face, which seemed older than how he had remembered it. The soap-streaked plate bounced sparks of light into his eyes and off the wall. He moved the plates around and the image was gone.

Snipe Paints & Chemicals

Tom Baxter approached the entrance of Snipe Paints & Chemicals. With its orange brick building and double arched windows, the sounds that came out of it were part of the high street's noise and bustle and a lot of men had been employed there from the Nichol over the years. The whiff was something rotten and you could smell it all the way down to St Leonards even on a Sunday.

Wearing paint covered overalls, the foreman waited in the large entrance hall with his arms crossed. He was surrounded by boys of varying ages, the clanging and scraping of machines filled the huge space and men walked around with paint cans, sacks and buckets.

'Welcome!'

All the children looked up. With Lady raised, Arthur Snipe stood atop an iron bridge overlooking the factory. Tom's eyes narrowed.

'This is your first day at Snipe Paints & Chemicals and we want to say how happy we are for you to join our family. Jon, the foreman, will show you around and I shall be meeting you all individually as the day progresses. Over to you, Jon!'

'Thank you, Mr Snipe. Now, first we need to get your uniforms and then we can begin the tour.'

He pointed to a mound of clothes by the entrance. As Tom searched in the stinking pile for something that might fit him, he asked himself in which way this was different to prison. He didn't have an answer.

When they had all changed into the work clothes, Jon pointed to the right of the entrance where there was a large windowless corridor. An array of machines stood on either side and men rotated pulleys as white powder was poured into vats of bubbling liquid.

'This is the mixing stage.'

The next group of workers pulled levers up that forced poo-like material into huge mixing tanks, the next group swirled huge oars around the dark liquid as it was then poured through brass pipes out to the waiting cans. There was one line for white, one for dark blue and one for dark red. The spirity smell burnt your eyes and nose hairs.

'This is where the paint's coloured, extruded and placed into cans.'

Holding their noses, the children shuffled along to a broader room that led out to a glass-covered courtyard and the machine noise quietened. Most of the workers here sat at long tables with paper sheets and wide paint brushes. Five horses stood by eating as carriages were piled high with the pots.

'This is where the labels are added, the paint stored, or taken away for delivery.'

A boy with a head of blonde curly hair, pointed with his sleeve covered hand to a set of dark blue double doors leading to another long room at the back of the factory wall.

'What's in there?'

'That's where the chemicals are made, out of bounds to the likes of you, son. Very dangerous. Very dangerous.'

'Now, one more thing. Every Wednesday afternoon Mr Snipe is to be served his mutton soup at his desk. There is a roster for the job on the pantry wall. Whoever's turn it is will be given some soup of their own and is permitted to eat with Snipe at his desk. This is to show how fair Mr Snipe is, and it gives him a chance to find out about the factory directly from you. Now, any questions?'

'What if we don't want to eat with him?'

The small sea of children parted to reveal Tom Baxter with his arms folded.

'I would strongly advise that you take Mr Snipe up on his kind gesture.'

'I don't like mutton. It's smelly,' Tom replied.

All the other children started laughing and copying Tom's voice and repeating the words *I don't like mutton, it's smelly, I don't like mutton, it's smelly.*

'Shut up, you lot!' Jon shouted.

All the children stopped, and a metallic tapping could be heard high up, as Arthur Snipe appeared on his walkway.

'What seems to be the trouble, Jon, everything all right?'

'Perfectly fine, Mr Snipe, I was just finishing the tour.'

'Jolly good. Jolly good.'

The boys muttered quietly to themselves.

'Now, let's get started!'

All the boys were sorted into groups and given a section of the process to work on along the long line of machines. Tom was put at the end with a man with clumps of missing hair who looked no more than 20 years old. He showed Tom how to cut the labels out with a broad metal cutting machine, apply the foul smelling fishglue and rotate the can on the bench in one swift movement. They sat side by side and Tom copied the way he worked. The chemical glue made his eyes hurt and his throat burn, his head felt fast and floaty all at once. Soon he was rhythmically cutting, painting and sticking. It felt as if his hands had become like a machine and that he wasn't in control of them. By midday he had glued over a hundred cans and they sat in a neat stack behind his bench.

After how long, Tom didn't know, Jon rang a loud bell and all the workmen stopped for the tea break and mugs were handed around as they all filed into the break room. Tom was passed a mug and the tea-taste mingled with the gluey smell in the back of his throat. In the break room a rusty stove hissed away underneath a big brass clock. Tom's eyes focussed and unfocussed on the clockface and it became a giant pocket watch, dangling and swinging from side to side. One of the clock hands turned into Arthur Snipe's nose and then into his whole face. The clock grinned at him, licking its lips and then blew Tom a kiss. This face dissolved and then transformed into his mother's, kindly looking down at him. The break bell rang once more and the workers sprang into action. The clock in the break room was always ten minutes fast. The clock in the factory, ten minutes slow.

As Tom prepared for his next shift, he looked to the end of the warehouse and saw Arthur Snipe and Theodore Hush with another man walking towards the blue double doors. His eyes followed them as they opened the padlock and entered what looked like a small corridor of some sort from which not one glint of light came. Hush poked his head out of the doors and then slammed them closed. Then a slice of light from under the doors appeared. Tom turned his head to try to listen to what they were saying but could only hear muffled conversation through the thick closed doors. The bald worker struck Tom's arm and fixed his eyes and shook his head slowly.

The Royal Pharmaceutical Society

Just three months after the boys had been released from the court, Arthur Snipe stood in front of his glass in the bedroom of his house at Annette Crescent. He adjusted his collar, pulled down his waistcoat and flicked a speck of dust from his shoulder. He tipped his head back and searched his nostrils for hairs, turned in profile and sucked in his stomach. Checking the time, he glanced out of the window down to the waiting coach and clapped his watch closed.

In the street, the whiteness of the crescent looked even brighter this autumn morning. As the front door opened, the driver jumped down from his coach and let Snipe into the cabin. Arthur Snipe sat back with a smile. The coach sped along City Road, and he looked at the little people below, dragging their wheelbarrows, flower ladies shouting, coachmen tending to their horses. With his eyes closed, Snipe breathed in the cold air as they trundled south to Clerkenwell and on to Rosebury Avenue. Holborn approached and he tugged down his waistcoat once more as the building came into view.

Inside the Royal Pharmaceutical Society, a hundred years of British medical history stared down from the portraits adorning the walls of the large oval drawing room. The light flooding in from Bloomsbury Square cast shadowed window frames over the vast oriental carpet. The waiter passed Snipe a Champagne glass. Gathering around the large central table, the physicians and lawmakers took turns signing the scrolled document. With pursed lips, Sir William Horace, Health Minister, stood to address the room.

'Today marks a new day in the management of controlled substances within our *United* Kingdom. For too long, the unfettered access to addictive opioids has undermined the lives of the working people. The poverty that so many face will now be eased by restricting the distribution and controlling the sale of these medicines, via a stringent new licencing system.'

'Thanks to responsible civic-minded businessmen like Arthur Snipe here.'

He gestured over to Snipe who had already drained his Champagne and was fiddling with the empty glass.

'These dangerous drugs will be given proper legal controls and working people up and down the country will have the protection they need.'

He raised his glass.

'To the Pharmacy Act!'

'The Pharmacy Act!'

Down in the square, the coaches were waiting. The two physicians held on to the shaking cabin as Arthur Snipe stepped up and squeezed himself between them. They looked out of their respective windows.

'Arthur Snipe. Snipe Paints and Chemicals. Where're we off to then, gents?'

Snipe offered his hand, which they both ignored.

'*Wiltons*, I believe,' the man to Snipe's left answered, in a strangled tone.'

'Driver, 'op it! We're off to *Wheel Tons*. Wherever that is.'

They pulled away, and the convoy of coaches proceeded south to Mayfair.

As soon as they arrived, Arthur Snipe jumped off the carriage and barged in ahead of the group as they entered the restaurant. The maître d' took his coat and cane and he was ushered into the private dining room with the others. Fishy garlic and quiet conversation filled the air.

Waiters stood at each corner of the intimate room, with napkin-draped arms, as the twelve men sat in coral coloured velvet seats. The plates and glassware sparkled under the electric light centrally suspended by a chain from the ceiling. Wall-mounted lighting illuminated oil paintings of rural scenes and classical themes of war and heroism.

Snipe looked around the room and noticed the way everyone sat. A sort of stiff deportment it was. As if a broom was stuck up one's arsehole good and proper. He sat up and spread his shoulders back in the same way the best he could, without his stomach forcing him further backwards from the table edge.

Sir Horace gestured for everyone to stand, and Snipe looked from side to side and copied their movements as the waiters moved in unison and poured the Champagne.

'Gentlemen! You are here to enjoy the best Mayfair has to offer. You have, as they say, earned your supper or *lunch* in this case.'

A titter of laughter.

'After two long years, we have finally passed our law!'

They raise their glasses once more.

'Might I recommend the Beef Wellington, a personal favourite of mine here and the claret is excellent. Gentlemen!'

'Sir Horace!'

They all sipped at their glasses and took their seats, accompanied by the sound of tinkling silverware. As Snipe sat, he tucked his napkin into his neck collar, looked around and quickly untucked it, placing it neatly on his lap as the others had.

'So, Mr Snipe, you are *in paint*. Is business good?' a sphincter-mouthed Junior Health Minister asked as he slowly caressed the tiniest piece of butter on a morsel of bread.

'Business *is* good, yes. We've been going for ten years now. We supply the whole of London and the Southeast as well as parts of the North. It allows me to indulge my passion for the racing.'

'Ah, Ascot.'

'No. Walthamstow. I like the gee-gees too, though,' Snipe answered, as he placed an entire bread roll in his mouth.

'Oh, quite.'

'And what exactly is your *role* in today's proceedings, if you don't mind me asking?'

'Godfrey's cordial. Distribution and storage. Secure storage. If you get my drift.'

'Indeed. Very much needed. That tincture has been the bane of many a family. Pure addictive poison. I am glad to see it will be in a safe pair of hands at last,' the health minister answered.

A man with a narrow face, as if it had been compressed in a vice, joined in the conversation.

'It's so exciting to have someone here from *the East*. From what I gather, the Old Nichol is quite the place. The Morrison book is a frightful read. Is it really as dangerous as they say?'

'It's safe as long as you keep your wits about you. Carry a cosh and such like. As a matter of fact, I heard of a man's dog recently being murdered. Just over a debt.'

There was an audible intake of breath as more members of the group started to bend forward to listen.

'How ghastly. Who would do such a thing?' the physician asked.

'Well, I know. Not *all* people are *good* people, are they? Not like us here. However, there are rules you know.'

'Rules?' the narrow-faced physician asked.

'Well, in *the East*, as you call it. There's *rules*. If someone crosses you. Takes something that was yours...'

Snipe was holding a bread roll in one hand, squeezing a knife in the other. Crumbs of bread falling all over his chest.

'You have to teach them a lesson, don't you? Pay them back.'

Snipe noticed the whole table was leaning towards him. He softened his delivery with a benign smile.

'I mean, there is a form of justice in the Old Nichol and other such environs.'

'Yes. Fascinating. *An eye for an eye,*' the physician whispered across the table and winked.

'Well, a *dog's* eye in this case. Or so I heard,' Snipe added.

'Will you be having the Wellington, Mr Snipe?'

'No, I've already got a pair of boots.'

A silence descended.

Snipe then clicked his fingers.

'Here, waiter. You got any lamb?'

A waiter lurched forward.

'Yes, sir, the Barnsley Chops are very good, sir.'

'Good, I'll have that, and have you any beer in this place? This Champagne is making me well parched.'

'Right away, sir.'

He then caught the eye of a young ferrety man opposite who had been listening in to the conversation. Observing him. Snipe couldn't tell if it was approvingly or suspiciously. The man spoke across the table.

'Mr Snipe. You are *the* Arthur Snipe from the papers?'

He had a stuttering way of talking, despite his confidence and poise.

'Ah, that. Yes. Guilty as charged. Poor little urchins they was. It's not their fault. It's rough on the young uns. I like to give them a chance, you know.'

'Richard Roughton. Pleased to meet you, Arthur.'

'Likewise.'

'Is it true you like to help these children? I mean with work. They are really working in your shop?'

'Oh, it was nothing, honestly. Yes, indeed, I have twenty workers. However, I must correct you. It isn't a shop but a factory. We manufacture and store paint, you see. For the trade.'

'Ah, my mistake. I apologise. Paint you say?'

'Yes, the finest paint this side of Watford. We do all three ranges. Two types of red, which is very advanced. We're using the newest methods and have contracts with dye makers in

Leeds, Manchester and Nottingham. In fact, we've started to make the... chemicals on-site.'

'Fascinating. Mr Snipe, would you be interested in joining me for a drink. In private. After luncheon? I may have an interesting proposition for you.'

'What's your game then?' Snipe asked.

'My *game*, Arthur, is sculpture and architecture. I'm a draftsman. I'm building a large concert hall near the South Kensington Museum, and we are running into... problems. It's all rather fraught actually.'

'I'm pleased to offer my services, Mr Roughton. Do you know a place we could discuss this in detail?'

'My club. It's just around the corner.'

'Look forward to it.'

As the courses arrived, Arthur Snipe became more inebriated. He noticed how the others were enthralled by his appetite but began not to care. No matter how much food came, the plates were dispatched one by one. He had been given his own breadbasket by the time the third course arrived and had polished that off too. When the plates for the final course were collected, the cigar box was presented, and Snipe selected one of the biggest and sniffed it. He felt a hand on his shoulder.

'Mr Snipe, shall we adjourn to the Athenaeum? My carriage is just outside.'

Richard Roughton was already wearing his hat and coat.

'You can take that with you,' Richard said, pointing.

Snipe inhaled the vegetal aroma of the unlit cigar and then slipped it into his waistcoat pocket.

The Athenaeum Club

Arthur Snipe and Richard Roughton sat opposite each other in the coach. Snipe eyed the man. Assessing. Weighing up the potential. As he did, Richard stared back with narrow eyes that seemed deep in thought.

'Have you been before?' Roughton asked.

The club? No. Not really my game. I'm more a pub kind of bloke.'

'Indeed. Well, nevertheless. I think you will like it, Mr Snipe.'

'I'm sure I will, Mr Roughton.'

'Call me Richard.'

He leaned towards Snipe and squeezed his knee.

'Beef Wellington!' Snipe blurted out, backing away into his seat.

'Excuse me, Arthur?'

'What is it?' Snipe asked.

'Fillet Beef wrapped in pastry. It is rather good. Why?'

'Sounds a bit... different.'

'You should try it. You might *like it.*'

Snipe attempted to move further back in his seat and was relieved as the coach slowed to pull into Pall Mall. He could see the entrance lit by flames with four columns over the door. A gold statue of a woman holding a spear looked down on Snipe from above. Snipe gripped his cane handle.

'Home from home,' Roughton exclaimed.

They were greeted by top-hatted porters who swung the doors open. Roughton led the way and Snipe stumbled in after him.

Inside the main entrance, guests ambled this way and that, and black-suited staff busied themselves. Roughton and Snipe seemed to be the youngest there.

They were led across to one of the carpeted drawing rooms, replete with low-lit chandeliers and leather armchairs. As they entered, a man with a white, feather-like moustache flicked his newspaper and looked up from it. In another corner, four men who had been leaning forward talking, stopped and sat back to toast with whisky glasses raised. The vast space was a gas of cigar and pipe smoke.

'Ah, here we are,' Roughton showed Snipe his seat by the fire.

'Much obliged,' Snipe replied flicking his jacket up from behind him as he sat.

'Are you a gin, brandy or whisky man?'

Snipe raised his finger and started to answer but was cut off.

'Let me guess.'

He looked Snipe up and down and his eyes narrowed.

'Whisky! I am right, aren't I?'

'Guilty as charged,' Snipe answered.

A waiter seemed to appear out of nowhere, perhaps from behind a curtain or a plant.

'A bottle of Lagavulin and two glasses please.'

The waiter just nodded to Roughton and left.

'Very nice place,' Snipe said as he looked around.

'Yes, I'm not keen on *most* of the clubs, but this one is a little different. Women are allowed for one thing.'

'You mean whores?'

Roughton, who had just taken a sip of water, spat out a mouthful with laughter. Snipe looked around not realising there had been a joke.

Roughton started coughing and was forced to take another swig.

'Mr Snipe, you are a real character, I give you that. What I meant was, women are allowed as *guests*. Most clubs don't allow it. The Athenaeum is more open. Progressive.'

'Ah, of course,' Snipe said.

The silence was broken by the waiter who brought a whisky decanter, two lowball glasses and a jug of water on a silver platter. Generous measures were poured, the glasses passed to each of them, and the bottle placed precisely in the centre of their table.

'Mr Snipe, the world is changing you know.' Roughton sighed as he stared into the fireplace.

'Oh? In what way?'

'Everything from engineering to working methods. Industrialisation. To business. It's becoming faster. More *dynamic*. The new century is just around the corner, and we are hardly ready for what is coming.'

Snipe just looked around the room and slurped at his liquor.

'Which brings me to my problem. We are having *issues* with our paint supplier presently. Manchester is becoming a difficult place to do business at the moment. Are you aware of the unions?'

'Not really.'

'Good. The Labour movement is becoming a thorn in our side, so we need options. Are you able to offer one, Mr Snipe?'

'Of course. We are ready when you are.'

'Mr Snipe, I want you to write down a figure on this napkin for supplying paint for our little concert hall here in Kensington. Think long and hard. Then make me an offer.'

'How much paint do you require, Mr Roughton?'

'The main auditorium is 185 feet wide by 219 feet long. You can start with quoting for that, and we'll take it from there, yes?'

He wrote down measurements on the napkin and slid it over to Snipe. Snipe swallowed as quietly as he could.

'Take your time. I appreciate it will be a lot to consider,' Roughton concluded.

Snipe noticed Roughton had been looking over his shoulder every so often when they had been talking. The meeting concluded, a man came over to the table and stood near to Richard. Without a word, he looked down to him with a smile and something passed between them, a secret understanding a silent greeting of sorts.

Roughton stood and shook Snipe's hand softly.

'I will be in one of the private rooms. Your offer, tonight, if possible. Enjoy the club and relax. Be my guest and we shall talk later.'

'Righto, Richard. You go and...'

But he had already walked off. Snipe's eyes followed them. Roughton tipped the waiter and gestured to where Snipe was sitting and gave him a wave before leaving the drawing room.

Snipe sat back and lit his cigar, rolling it between his fingers until it was good and orange. He pulled out his pencil and began to make calculations on the napkin. His hand was shaking as he did so, his heart beating fast. He poured another large whisky, sat back and thought. Then he began making more calculations in a notebook, feverishly scribbling and crossing out numbers, adding subtracting, refining.

Figures floated in and out of Snipe's mind, in front of his eyes. They wafted past the fireplace, out of the window; rose over to South Kensington and flew into a grand concert hall, into tubas and trumpets, circling a string section and twisting around the conductor's wand, before rising once again to the huge ceiling. Numbers and fractions and pounds and shillings danced above Snipe's head as the symphony reached a crescendo.

Snipe was awoken by someone shaking his shoulder. He leapt up from his chair. The last of the orange embers were being suffocated at the base of the fireplace and most of the gaslights in the drawing room were off. Richard was staring down at him, his necktie undone.

'I thought it best I brought some coffee.'

One of the waiters handed over a steaming silver jug surrounded by cups and saucers and removed the empty whisky decanter.

'My apologies, Richard. I must have nodded off,' Snipe said as he bunched his collar around his neck against the chill.

'Don't worry, Mr Snipe, it's not the first time here and it certainly won't be the last.'

He poured a coffee and passed it to Snipe and poured one for himself.

'So, have you thought about the costing? I hope you had time in between *naps*.'

'Yes, I have it right here. Mr Roughton, I have considered this project from all angles. All eventualities. It does seem an unusual job to me. I have factored in all of this when thinking about the cost and I hope it meets with your expectations.'

He slid the napkin over to Roughton who picked it up and looked over the numbers written in spikey but clear writing.

'Mmm, interesting.'

He retrieved a gold pencil from his inside pocket and made a few marks here and there, squinting over to Snipe every so often, then finally passing it back over to him.

Snipe looked down at the napkin and took a gulp of coffee. Then he looked up with a smile.

'Mr Roughton, I am not *unhappy*, but I am a little *confused*. These figures are higher than the ones I presented. Much higher.'

'A *procurement* fee is included, Mr Snipe. Her Majesty requires it for all works related to the Crown Lands. The hall was originally in the name of Prince Albert, until he passed on, of course. God bless his soul.'

'Yes, indeed, God rest his soul. So, this procurement fee would be going to... Her Majesty directly?'

'Well, yes, eventually. But first it goes to me. For safe keeping. I am Chairman of the Procurement Department for Arts and Crafts. You understand this is a matter of the Crown and there are rules and procedures to be followed. But don't worry about the detail. Leave all that to me.'

'So, how much off the whole amount?'

'Thirty per cent.'

Snipe looked back at the figures and sipped his coffee once more.

'Mr Roughton, I am very grateful for the chance to work on such a project, but the fee is rather low now it is minus the thirty. It's a little *off* what I had in mind, shall we say.'

Roughton sat forward and placed his coffee cup on its saucer.

'Mr Snipe, Arthur, you have *children* working in your factory. Possibly one of the few still operating in London of this size. Do you *really think* I chose your fucking company because of the quality of your paint. Come on be realistic. This is a fantastic opportunity for your business. Snipe Paint & Chemicals wins Albert Hall contract. Think of the prestige. The honour, *the publicity*. Just shake on it. Now, there's a good chap.'

Roughton sat back, lifted his cup and sipped the tiniest amount of coffee from the edge of it before placing it back on the saucer.

Snipe's fist crackled as it clenched under the table, but he remained calm above it.

'*Twenty*. Which brings us to...'

Snipe scribbled the figures down.

'This.'

He slid the amended napkin back over to Roughton.

'Ah. You don't give up that easily, do you, Arthur? *Twenty-five.*'

'Done,' Arthur replied, spat into his palm and offered it over to Roughton who ignored it and just took another sip from his coffee.

'I shall have my secretary draft the paperwork and send it over by tomorrow lunchtime. Can I get you a coach?'

Vanessa

Since the court case, Tom and Mr Tipps's relationship had changed. He wouldn't keep eye contact with Tom like before. Now he usually made work for himself in the storeroom and shuffled about re-arranging books that didn't need re-arranging. Every now again he'd poke his head out to see what Tom was doing, whilst keeping his distance. Tom didn't know if it was Mr Tipps looking after him or making sure he wasn't nicking anything. However many times Tom tried to explain how the events had taken place, Mr Tipps remained suspicious. Tom felt himself lucky that he was even allowed into the shop anymore.

Like any other weekday, the shop bell rang. The crunch of horse hooves entered as the door opened and receded as it closed. A slice of sun cut through a gap in the shop curtain and Tom watched her silhouette moving in the dust held there.

As if sensing his stare, she turned, raising her hand to shield her eyes from the sunshine. Tom ducked below his fortress of books. She turned back to the front counter.

'Good afternoon, Mr Tipps, I am here to collect a book that was ordered by my father just a week ago. The details are here.'

Tom, carefully this time, peeked between two bookshelves. The girl was now in profile and her elegantly gloved hand passed over a slip of paper to Mr Tipps, who nodded and moved out of view to search for the book.

'Hello,' the girl said turning in Tom's direction once more.

The sound was friendly and soft like the way a child introduces herself to a stray dog. Tom stepped out into view and knocked a shelf of books over, bending down to collect them in a messy heap on top of a display table.

'Do you work here?' she asked

'No. Just read here.'

'How curious,' the girl answered, half laughing, her sausage-like curls bouncing on her shoulders.

'Mr Tipps lets me read here all day. I like reading.'

'So do I. What are you reading at the moment?'

'Thunder and Lightnin'. It's my favourite.'

'Oh, what's it about?'

'It's about how lightning is made, electricity, science and that. It's very mysterious. Did you know that globular lightning can enter a house?'

'What's globular lightning?'

'Look, I'll show you.' Tom gestured for her to come towards him.

The girl craned her neck, stood on tip toes to look for Mr Tipps beyond his counter, shrugged her shoulders and stepped towards Tom.

'What's your name, boy?'

'Tom. Tom Baxter. What's yours?'

'Vanessa Bell.'

'Pleased to meet you, Vanessa Bell.'

'Likewise, Tom Baxter.'

As Tom showed her the first pages of the book, he noticed how clean her fingernails were. He curled his underneath the book out of sight.

'What a peculiar book indeed. Are they stories or are they based on history?'

'Bit of both, Miss Bell.'

'Vanessa, *please.*'

'Bit of both, Vanessa *Please,*' Tom replied smiling.

Vanessa giggled and placed her hand over her mouth.

'You are a funny one.'

Mr. Tipps appeared from the back of the shop looking flustered.

'I hope he's not disturbing you, Miss.'

'Not at all. In fact, he seems to be one of your top salesmen.' Vanessa gestured to the book.

'*That's* where it is. Tom have you been hiding it?'

Mr Tipps showed the piece of paper to Tom. The words *Thunder and Lightning for Mr Bell* were scrawled across it.

'Sorry, Tom, this one's sold to the customer's father, I'm afraid.'

Tom's face fell as he handed the book over to Mr Tipps, who then handed it over to Vanessa, who then handed it back to Tom.

'I couldn't possibly take this from you.'

Mr Tipps then took the book and handed it back to Vanessa.

'Nonsense. I can always order another one for Tom to read.'

Vanessa then slowly handed the book back to Tom. Static electricity crackled as their hands accidentally touched across it. They looked at each other not quite knowing what was happening.

'No, this one belongs to Tom.' Vanessa's eyes sparkled.

'If you are absolutely sure, Miss. I wouldn't want there to be a delay for your father.'

'He has plenty of books, Mr Tipps, it can wait. How long should it take?'

'No more than a week, I would say. Perhaps less.'

'Well, that settles it then. The book stays with Tom and I'll return for another copy in a week's time. Is that agreed?'

All Tom could do was stand with his mouth open like a stuffed animal.

'Goodbye, *Tom Baxter*, I shall see you in a week.'

As Vanessa left the shop, Tom slowly walked to the window and his eyes followed as she made her way down the road. He continued to look; she became a spec as she walked further away. The spec became a dot and she was gone.

Tom sat with his back to the window, his heart beating as he turned to see if he could still see her.

Mr Tipps laughed to himself as a re-arranged the books Tom had disturbed.

'Looks like someone could do with a cup of tea.'

The Afternoon with Vanessa

The following week in Mr Tipps's bathroom, Tom scraped with the nail brush, the basin full. Soap suds spilled over the edge making a dark water stain on his shirt. He nervously dabbed away with a towel and combed his hair down in the bathroom glass, noticing he had a blue streak of paint running down one side of his face. He desperately scraped with the soap and rinsed but it wouldn't move. Giving up, he rubbed his teeth with powder and rinsed again. The shop bell tinkled. Tom's heart skipped in a most queer way.

Tom peered through the gap in the bathroom door and saw Mr Tipps who stepped back to fetch the book for her.

Tom, lurking in the Theology section near the bathroom door, casually cast his eyes over the spines: Morals and Virtues by Simon R. Pinkerton; The Bible and its Attributes by Marcelle de Berniour; The Bible by, well, lots of people apparently. He looked to his left to see if Vanessa had noticed him. She hadn't, so he let out a gentle cough.

'Oh, hello. There you are.'

'Yes, I'm here.'

The words seemed stupid to Tom the minute they came from his mouth. He wanted to pull them back, but they stayed in the air uncomfortably.

'Have you been painting?'

'Oh, yes, it's my work...'

'How interesting, portraits or landscapes?'

'Houses.'

'Like Rowlandson!' said Vanessa.

'Is that another paint company?' Tom asked.

'You look... different,' said Vanessa.

'Oh, really. Good or bad?' Tom said smoothing his hair down.

'Good, actually. I was thinking, are you free this afternoon? Are you free at all?' she shyly placed he hands behind her back.

'Free? Mmm.'

'Yes, free. You know, are you available this afternoon? I wish to show you something.'

'Ah... free. Yes. Free, right. Yes. Free.'

'Tom, you repeated the word *free* many times. I am supposing that you are indeed free?'

'Yes, yes of course.'

'There's a place nearby that you would like, I think. It's not far. Just half a mile from here if that. Would you like to go with me?'

'I need to just check if I am in fact free. Just one moment please, Vanessa.' Tom raised his finger to the air.

He walked to the back of the shop to hide in the store room for a few seconds, where Mr Tipps was wrapping the book. He gestured silently with both hands for Tom to go. Tom paced about and smoothed his hair down, paced some more.

Vanessa appeared and saw what he was doing and giggled to herself.

'Tom, if it's not a good time, we could...'

'No! Free, I'm certainly free. *Yes.* I was just checking you know... with...'

Mr Tipps relieved the tension. 'Miss Bell, your book is here and it's all wrapped up and ready for you.'

'Thank you so much, Mr Tipps, what is the charge?'

'No, there's no charge, your father already paid for the book.'

'No, I meant for Tom's copy.'

Tom's heart skipped again.

'How generous. Did you hear that Tom, Miss Bell's buying your book for you?' Mr Tipps said.

'That'll be thirty-one, Miss Bell.'

Thirty bloody one? Tom thought.

'Vanessa, thank... thank you so much,' Tom said.

'My pleasure.'

'Thank you, Mr Tipps. Now, shall we go, Tom?'

Like a lamb, Tom just nodded and followed Vanessa out of the shop.

Out on the busy high street, the sound of carriage wheels blended with those of hawkers selling fruit and veg. The day was rare in its blue brightness and Tom squinted up to Vanessa as she walked by his side. Clouds like white mackerel stripes floated above her.

'So, Vanessa Bell, where are we going?'

'Patience, Tom. You will see. What do you know about electricity?'

'I know that Benjamin Franklin discovered it with his kite and it's in lightnin' and storms.' Tom smiled to himself.

'Well did you know it can be created and stored?'

Vanessa led Tom over to the left, past the next corner where the old lady sold heather wrapped in violet paper. Down Old Street was Hoxton Square and they walked into Coronet Street which wiggled deeper away from the main road.

'Here,' said Vanessa jumping to a stop.

At the far end, men were laying bricks, pushing wheelbarrows and climbing all over a new building. The sunlight made the front wall glow all orange like warm biscuits. He could see the workmen engraving some words over its grand arch.

'What queer words. I think they're spelling it all wrong, Vanessa. Look!'

'It's Latin, Tom. E quisquilia Lux et vis: from rubbish, light and power. Or more accurately, from dust, light and life. What's inside though is the part you'll like the most. Let's go.'

Vanessa hitched up her petticoat to avoid the sandy puddles and pulled Tom's hand towards the building's entrance.

As they approached, a man in overalls who seemed to be in charge nodded to Vanessa. She skipped over a plank and the man helped her over a wall into the building. Tom followed, looking around and above as he entered the large space. A group of pigeons fidgeted in a hole in the roof that let in the only sunlight.

'This is where they make electricity, Tom,' Vanessa shouted, her voice echoing above the din of the workmen.

'How?' Tom asked, breathing in the damp air.

'From rubbish. You see that opening there?'

'Yes.'

'Well, that's where they take the rubbish in and it goes all the way along here...' she jumped up to the far end of the big space, 'and take it here to be burnt. Then the heat turns these things which in turn creates electricity,' she said, moving her arms round in opposite circles.

Tom was doing his stuffed animal impression again.

'The electricity is stored here and then sent out to whoever needs it. That's it.'

'So, everyone knows 'bout this. It's not like top secret or nothin' like that?'

'Well, it is *new*. Brand new. But not top secret, no.'

'How you know so much about it, then, Vanessa?'

'My father designed it. He's an architect; sort of an engineer, too.'

'The rubbish comes all the way up the canal from Islington to Hackney, Shoreditch and here. Then boof! Like magic.' Vanessa snapped her fingers.

'Boof,' Tom replied copying her.

'Exactly.'

They stood in silence and Tom whistled, enjoying its echo as he imagined the finished building, electricity surging through the place and out to all the streets in London, the houses lighting one by one, spreading outwards like blood running through veins, *light and life*.

'Looks expensive though, who's payin' for it all, Vanessa?'

'That's easy, it's the London County Council. They are always looking for ways to help people. I can see why you are interested in electricity, Tom. It really will change everything, you know.'

'I wish they'd buy me a new 'ouse.'

'Well, funny you should say that, Tom, because they might well be doing that already.'

And with that, Vanessa pulled Tom's hand and led him out of the building sight and onto the sandy lane.

'Where we goin' now, Vanessa?'

'Next, I want to show you the future, Tom, your future.'

At the end of the lane, on the corner of Shoreditch High Street there stood a small shop window with a place of business attached. The letters LCC were above it. Tom was amazed he hadn't noticed it before.

Inside, there was a model of a house like the one in the toy shop, but this time the house was modern, simple and so big. As he bent to look down to the street level, he understood how big it really was because of the models of little people walking around its base. It seemed as if many families would live inside. It was like a big house where everyone could live. That was clever, it took up less room and meant that the streets could be wide with trees and bushes on the edges, these details were also there on the model. The orange bricks were ever so modern, and next to the windows, lighter coloured bricks went across and down in square patterns.

'I like it, Vanessa, what is it?'

'It's called the Boundary Estate and it's going to be built to replace the Old Nichol, Tom.'

'What's going to happen to the old houses?'

'They are going to knock them down, Tom.'

'What do you mean? Completely? Like smashed down?'

'Yes, Tom, and you'll have a new house. One of these.'

Tom moved his shoe around the orange sand, looked towards the Old Nichol and then back to the model in the window and felt the frayed edge of his sleeve.

'Are you sure everyone will be given one of these?'

'Yes, Tom. That's the whole idea. It's designed for people to have a decent house and to improve the lives of the working people.'

'Why d' you care so much about it then?'

'It's fair, don't you think, Tom? All people should be able to have a nice house of their own to live in. It should be a basic human right.'

'A human right,' Tom repeated, as if in a trance.

'Next, I want to show you my house.'

'Why?'

'What do you mean, Tom?'

'Why you being so nice an' that?'

'I... I like you, Tom...' Vanessa looked to the ground, 'and I don't have many, you know. Friends. Not like you anyway. Friends who are interested in electricity and lightning. The truth is you're a bit strange, Tom. So am I. There's one last thing I want you to see. No one in the world would be interested in it except for you and...'

Tom was now standing so close to her that she could feel his soft breath on her neck. He kissed her gently on the cheek.

'...me.'

Vanessa hailed a carriage on Curtain Road and pulled Tom up. As he sat back in the comfortable seat, he stared up at the driver as he carefully looked both ways and edged into the street.

'What's the matter, Tom?'

'Nothin', just thinking. So, where we goin' now?'

'Chelsea.'

'*Chelsea*. I'm lucky I met you, Vanessa.'

'Yes, you are,' she said, winking.

It was just then that he noticed a beauty mark just above the curve of her smile. He turned away and looked out of the carriage window to distract himself, hoping she hadn't noticed him staring.

As the carriage wheels spun down Commercial Street, the world outside sped past with them. The dark shops, like Hush's with all their wares stacked outside, started to dwindle in numbers and the buildings turned from dark brick to light marble. Into Fenchurch Street, its grand banks towering over all the working people dragging their wheelbarrows of chickens and goods to sell. As the road narrowed, Tom noticed a big tower with lines running up it and a gold coloured statue up top. It reminded him of a giant matchstick. As they stopped with other carriages blocked by the way, under his breath Tom quietly read out the words written on a shiny metal plate at the base of it.

'Near this site stood the shop belong-ing to Thomas Far-yn-er. The king's baker in which the great fire of September 1666 began.'

Maybe it *was* a giant matchstick after all. It made him think of all the history London held within its walls, that before the London he lived in, there had been a London so very different from the one he knew and that it had all disappeared and been replaced with this one. A new London.

'So, what's next on the tour, Vanessa Bell?'

'It's an invention. It's been lent to my father for safe-keeping.'

'Will I meet him, Vanessa, your father?'

'Oh, no, he's always far too busy. I hardly ever see him at all.' Vanessa looked out of the carriage and then down to her hands.

'Do you have brothers or sisters?'

'No, just me. In fact, I never knew my mother either. Just me and Papa.'

'I'm sorry.'

'I'm used to it, Tom.'

'So, what's the invention?'

'You'll see.'

The carriage was now hugging the side of the Thames as they moved Southwest past the City of London to Belgravia. Tom's dad always called it 'the Management Quarters'. Buckingham Palace rose into view and Tom raised his hand to his head in a salute, making Vanessa laugh. He bowed his head and started to wave his hand near the carriage window, as they passed the golden gates with its big-hatted guards. Vanessa pulled Tom's hand down and hid herself out of sight giggling away.

God save her gracious bum, God save her gracious bum, God save her bum..., Tom sang.

'Tom, *stop that*, you'll get us into trouble,' she laughed through her hand.

The driver was looking over his shoulder and laughing to himself as they approached Westminster, past the Houses of Parliament and the big new station at Pimlico and then back on to Chelsea embankment. To their right, the sun bounced light off the tall, white-framed windows of the new mansion flats facing the river. Vanessa smiled back to Tom as she caught him looking at her and shyly turned away as the coach turned right into Tite Street.

The coach stopped at a building with orange bricks very much like the model of the houses she had shown him earlier. Number 46 had two square white-topped pillars either side of the entrance and the words *The Tower House* were written on them. They walked up the clean marble steps leading to the shiny black door.

'You... *live* here, Vanessa?'

'Yes, just me and Pa.'

'You live in the whole building?'

'No, Tom, a flat. On the third floor. It's a maisonette.'

The hall had a black and white tiled floor, and it reminded Tom of a picture of a chess board he'd once seen at the bookshop. On the left, a gold framed glass made it look like there were two sculptures of a dancing lady either side of you, when really there was just one on the right. Vanessa led Tom up some stairs that had a soft carpet held in place by little metal feet. They walked up to a metal prison-looking box against the wall on the landing, at which point Tom hesitated.

'It's just a lift, Tom. They are new. You can walk the stairs but it's very tiring all the way up there.'

She unfolded the metal contraption's front, as it collapsed to one side like a Shoreditch shopfront, and got in.

'Look. See?' Vanessa said with both arms open, her heels clicking on the lift's wooden floor.

Tom stayed outside and poked his head in, looking to one side and up to the ceiling and then stepped carefully into the small, metal box. It wobbled slightly as he moved, and he gripped Vanessa's hand to steady himself. When she pressed the button for the third floor, it jolted and Tom held its edges as it juddered and crept up, revealing each floor through its bars.

'We've got some famous artists living here actually, seems to have become very popular with the bohemian set, you know.'

The lift wobbled to a stop.

'Ah, here we are. One more flight and it's us.'

Vanessa smashed the metal gate open to reveal a few more steps leading up to a front door.

Inside the flat's entrance, a narrow corridor with a long blue oriental carpet led to the right. Tom followed Vanessa and she guided him to a large drawing room with a grand piano to the left and huge windows overlooking a park. You could see so far across London that Tom imagined himself being able to see his own street. He squinted and could have sworn he saw his house and his mother putting out the washing.

'Tea?'

'Yes, please. Vanessa, how long have you lived here?' Tom asked, fiddling with a brass telescope by the window.

'Father bought it just last year when it was built.'

'You... you *own* it?'

'Yes, Tom. Now. Tea.'

A few minutes later, she returned with a tray on which a blue patterned teapot sat. Next to it, there were two matching cups and saucers and a pile of biscuits on a plate. Vanessa gestured for Tom to sit at a long, soft seat that seemed to have hundreds of pillows of all colours on it. As he sat, his small body disappeared into their velvety folds and his legs stood out, his scuffed shoes dangling. He bent forward and drank the tea carefully and copied the way Vanessa slowly ate her biscuits.

'Now, when you're finished we can see it.' Vanessa's eyes sparkling.

Vanessa sipped her cup and glanced at Tom before looking across Chelsea and beyond to Westminster and Central London. She thought of how calm he had been and how much she loved spending time with him.

'Shall we?'

As Tom finished his plate of biscuits and stuffed some more in his pocket, he climbed down, and Vanessa gestured to a smaller room off the hall.

Inside, the dim gaslight revealed a dark wood dining table with four empty chairs. As Tom came closer, he touched the tabletop which was covered in dust, wiped his greasy fingers together and his hand down his trouser side.

In the centre of the table a tall domed glass case sat that was similar to one you would see in an insect museum. But instead of insects it contained a miniature fairground ride, the type with horses for children to sit on as it goes round and round to organ music. It had small chains, like necklaces running up to a central point at the top to what looked like a big round bell. Tom had been on one with his dad in Bethnal Green when he was younger.

'It's a merry-go-round, Vanessa!'

'No, Tom. It's called a Tempest Prognosticator. It predicts storms and lightning.'

'How?'

Vanessa bent her body down to show Tom the object closer.

'You see those glasses?'

As Tom peered in, he noticed that the fairground horses weren't horses at all but glass jars. Each glass, six in total, had a measure of clear liquid and something small and black inside.

'They each contain a leech. When the storm approaches, the creatures move up and out of the water and tilt the whalebone piece here. You see the chains that link to the big bell at the top?'

'Yes.'

'Each one has a clapper attached at the top. The bigger the storm, the more the bell tinkles.'

'So, this *Tempist Proglosticator* really works, Vanessa?'

'Yes, Tom. I've seen it work every time.'

'Vanessa, I...'

'You what, Tom?' Vanessa smiled.

All Tom could do was stare at the machine and back at Vanessa.

'Why is it here?'

'Father knows the inventor, Mr Merryweather. I know, that is his real name, yes. It was shown at the Great Exhibition and he's presenting it to some investors here in London. Apparently, it was inspired by a line in Edward Jenner's poem, *Signs of Rain*.'

The leech disturbed is newly risen; Quite to the summit of his prison. As she spoke, Tom watched her distorted face on the other side of the glass, her green eyes stretching, moving back into place and stretching again. Her auburn hair turning to a flame red, waving outward as if blown by the wind or floating in water. The leeches seemed to be wiggling and gently peering up to them, the way new-borns recognise their parents when they awaken.

That afternoon, Tom and Vanessa talked most enthusiastically for hours about lightning, science and, of course, leeches. The sun dipped over the west London skyline, covering its brittle horizon with a soft orange glow that blended to dark brown as the day became evening, and evening to night. Vanessa arranged for a coach and their hands touched briefly as she helped Tom up to his seat. As the coach left, they looked at each other for as long as they could until the horses swept Tom back to Shoreditch.

The School of Mr Tipps

The following afternoon, full of energy after his day with Vanessa, Tom started to ask Mr Tipps to help him with his book more regularly. He had begun to trust Tom once again and things went back to how they were before: the daily routines, the conversations about books and reading.

Some of the scientific words were difficult and Mr Tipps did his best explaining them by using other books and drawing diagrams and pictures on paper. He was a quite a good teacher, actually, if a little impatient.

Soon they were conducting experiments in the back room using water jars, ribbon and salt. Some worked better than others. One time Tom almost set fire to a first edition, another, Mr Tipps got his eyebrows singed off, but eventually the experiments became more and more successful and Tom's book became clearer to him. He realised that it was more about history, the milestones of when lightning had been discovered and small sections detailing theories about how man-made electricity related to it.

After eight months, Tom could understand most of the pages and read them aloud fluently. In the bookshop they began to hold evenings where Tom read from his book, Mr Tipps and Vanessa each took turns to read out something that they had been reading.

He then began to read anything and everything he could get his hands on. If Mr Tipps couldn't find a book when customers asked for something, he was sure that Tom probably had it. Every time this happened, he went hunting around the shop for Tom, who was usually to be found reading and scribbling away in some little corner of the shop. One evening Tom plucked up the courage to ask him something. The question had been burning within him for the best part of a year.

'Mr Tipps, can I ask you something?'

'Yes, what is it this time, Tom?' he said smiling.

'Can I work here? You know, like as a job?'

Tipps removed his glasses and carefully placed them on his book and breathed out.

'Look, Tom, I just can't afford it. Wish I could, mate. This shop isn't cheap to rent at all. I only make a small amount of profit as it is. Some months I just break even. I'm sorry, Tom. Look, I promise if I need an assistant, *you* will be the first to hear about it. You practically run the place anyway. You know where all the books are, all the sections, all the rarities. All the nooks and crannies.'

Tom looked back down to his reading.

'Mr Tipps, did you know that they can make and store electricity now?'

'I had read something about that, yes. It's near here, I think, London County Council.'

'Yes, Vanessa showed me.'

Mr. Tipps simply looked back to his book.

'Do you think we will all have it?'

'Electric light, Tom?'

'Yes, you know in every home. Maybe even here in this shop?'

'I'm sure of it, Tom, but I don't know how soon that will happen, mate.'

Tom flicked through his book again.

'You know I understand, don't you?'

'The book, Tom? I know. You've made a lot of progress. Perhaps I should become a full-time teacher. I'd probably make more money.'

'No, I mean the job. I understand it's hard to employ me. I don't mind. I hope I can still stay here though. I mean stay and read an' that.'

'Course you can, mate. You are *always* welcome to stay as long as you want, Tom. Tell you what. Why don't you read me something from your book as I get ready to go home. How does that sound?'

As Tom read, Mr Tipps packed away his ledger and duster, and walked to the pantry making sure that he could hear Tom to correct him when needed.

—Globular Lightning—

Globular lightning appears to have a special liking for gutters for the pipes which discharge the rain water from our roofs.

It is passionately fond of gas pipes and other metallic objects with which houses are furnished. On the 10th of September, 1845, a ball of lightning presented itself at the threshold of a kitchen owned by a farmer situated in the village of Salagnac. Luckily for him, he had been electrified one day on the Champs Elysées for two sous.

He had learnt to respect the mysterious fluid and its shocks; he allowed the ball to pass by. It was fortunate indeed that he did so, for a few seconds later the treacherous sphere exploded violently in a neighbouring stable.

'So, lightning is attracted by metal pipes, the way electricity is conducted by metal?'

'Seems so, Tom.'

'And I suppose if water is there, that might make the electricity even more *volatiled*?' Tom asked.

'*Volatile*, Tom. It's an adjective not a passive verb. But, yes, it would. It all sounds rather dangerous, so don't get any ideas about doing that here, you'll burn the place down. Now get ready I have to lock up, my omnibus is coming. We can continue with your reading tomorrow.'

The Boundary Estate September 2022

A pizza delivery driver darted past. A giant daddy longlegs flapped out of the bike's path and settled onto one of the recycled bathtubs containing plants and herbs artfully arranged at the base of one of the blocks in the Boundary Estate.

The bath started to vibrate and the insect flew off. Inside the tub, the surface of loose dirt shook like a small earthquake.

The plants began to slowly wave, grow, wither and die, grow and wave again. Dots of pollen dust, as if squeezed from dry mushroom heads, ascended in slow motion and gathered two inches above the dirt's surface, forming a haze of crimson and ochre like the gases on a distant moon.

A discarded KFC box rolled away and dispersed the sea of red mist to reveal the white face of a broken sculpture buried in the dark earth. The black eyes opened, and the face rose up, the vibrating sound intensifying. A bleached hand gripped the edge of the bath, the shape of a body appeared from the earth and pulled itself out, plant roots and mud dust falling away.

In the wall of one of the residential blocks, there was a small opening the size of just two or three bricks or more. A bone-white face appeared from within the dark hole. Eyes as black as coal looked left, looked right, then disappeared into the darkness in a puff of orange brick dust.

Snipe Paint and...

Behind the blue doors, Arthur Snipe with his hands behind his back, looked proudly along the dark corridor with Hush by his side. At one end, crates of Godfrey's cordial sat. The long thin space was filled with bubbling glass tubes and flasks mounted on dark metal spider legs above gas burners. The smell, burnt and sour.

A man with a white mask, matching hair and laboratory coat passed Hush and Snipe face coverings of their own which they quickly donned. He guided them along the length of pipes until they reached the far end where a black liquid squeezed out of a droopy pipe and collected in a large glass bowl underneath.

'Sir, as requested, the Godfrey's will be stored in the lockups and an excess amount has been kept back to make the street product here.'

'So, how's all this work then?' Snipe asked.

As the chemist spoke, he pointed along the line of pipe and tubes.

'The Godfrey's is heated to make a concentration here and mixed with pure alcohol and morphine along here. The mixture is then simmered, and the condensation taken off here. The product is secreted at this point and collected at the end where it dries and hardens. The ratio of Godfrey's to product will be approximately ten to one. It will be extremely potent as requested.'

'How will they consume the 'frey's?' Snipe asked.

It is water-soluble and can also be eaten, I suppose. Smoked too.'

'When will it be ready?'

'Six stones' weight will be processed by the end of this week. Enough for a year's supply by my estimation. The first batch is already synthesised.'

He lifted up the hardened oil-like substance pressed into a flat metal tray and placed it into his brown leather Gladstone bag. They left the laboratory and Hush carefully padlocked the door. As they walked through the busy factory up to Snipe's office, the chemist continued to speak discreetly.

'I recommend that you keep each package in jute pouches. They will protect the material when transported.'

The chemist presented the piece of rough sacking cut out into a rectangle that could be folded over to form a square.

'There is enough jute in here for this batch,' he lifted the briefcase slightly.

'Good. The legal stuff's to be distributed to all the pharmacies by Monday morning.'

'Indeed. Will that be all, sir?'

'That's it. You can go. Make sure you keep monitoring the laboratory.'

'Sir.'

The chemist carefully passed the briefcase over to him.

Inside his office, Snipe opened his pocketknife and began slicing out equal portions of the black tar-like 'frey's, placing them on a weighing scale. Hush sat on the opposite side of the desk, edging the scissors around the jute. After some time, a pile of square, woolly brown pouches was spread out on the desk. Both the men washed their hands leaving dark oily stains all over the basin rim.

'Three hundred, divided by six, lads, so that's fifty each. Manchester, York, Birmingham, Leeds, Liverpool, Nottingham. Perfect. Here are the prices. Make sure all are agreed in advance.'

Hush took down the figures in a brown ledger as he spoke.

'Each month, after a lad brings my soup, I'll give them ten to start off. Each lad will go one month at a time just to be on the safe side. I'll personally put word ahead to the men collecting the deliveries. They are to meet at the train stations only. None of my boys are to get involved after the delivery takes place. They are to come straight back with the money; the 'frey's goes up with the lads and the money comes down with them. Is that clear?'

'Of course, Mr Snipe.'

'One more thing. We need the lads to think the deliveries are to do with the paint. Call the packages *special paint dyes.* New materials, top secret, I don't fucking know, you think of something. You're good at that, Hush. Send the first lad on the list up today so we can get started.'

'Understood.'

Snipe counted ten packages and scooped back the remainder, turned the hefty lock on the safe behind his desk and placed them inside.

Below, the factory was in full swing, with all its smashing and scraping, as the curly-haired blonde boy collected the tea tray from the pantry. On it two bowls sat, accompanied by two rolls, spoons and napkins. He heaved the tray up the metal staircase, being careful not to spill anything as he went.

At the top of the stairs Theodore Hush stood.

'Oi, Curly.'

'Yes, sir.'

'You can go straight in. Also, he needs to give you some paint materials to take up to...'

He cast his pencil over his ledger.

'York.'

'What for?'

'Never you mind what for, just do as he says.'

Hush knocked and heard a muffled invitation. Behind his desk, Arthur Snipe neatened his collar and waistcoat. Hush opened the door and ushered the boy into the office.

'Ah, here we are. Soup time! And our very first *important* meeting. Put it down there, son, and take a seat.'

The boy reached up to place the tray on top of a mass of papers on Snipe's desk and sat opposite him. Curly just sat looking around the room swinging his legs under the wooden chair.

Behind the desk there was a huge double window with the curtain pulled aside. He could see the large courtyard below and hear the paint clattering onto the carriages. Just below the window to Snipe's side was a huge metal box, the corners scraped and chipped.

'Well go on, lad, don't wait for me. This is good stuff you know. Make you big and strong.'

Snipe preceded to inhale his soup with deep slurps and licks, as he tore into his roll and swished it around the thick liquid.

The boy did the same, pieces of meat dropping down as he ate.

With a full mouth, Snipe began to talk.

'So, boy, how are you enjoying the exciting world of paint?'

'Alright, suppose. Gets a bit smelly.'

'Good, good. How's Jon treating you?'

'We get tea breaks an' that.'

'Yes, of course, lad. We run a fair workshop. What about the other workers?'

'Whatcha mean, Mr Snipe?'

'Well, any complaints like from older workers, line managers? We want everyone to be happy at Snipe's, don't we?'

'Well, there was one man, Jim, I think his name is. He said the hours is too long and he said you was a cunt.'

'A cunt? Really that *is* interesting. Those words exactly? You want some of my roll, lad?'

'Thanks, Mr Snipe.'

The boy grabbed the bread and chewed into it.

'Yes. Cunt, he said. Dunno why.'

'Good. Good. That *is* very useful, lad. Thank you. Anything else?'

'No, don't think so, Mr Snipe.'

They finished their soup in silence until Snipe pushed his plate aside.

'I need to explain something to you, Curly. We have a special dye that needs taking up to York. Sort of important *business* mission. Are you up to the job, lad?'

Snipe gestured with his spoon which flicked soup all over the desk.

'Yes, Hush said.'

He handed the boy a sack with two handles that you could hold over your shoulder.

'In here is the important paint chemical. Tomorrow, you need to go to Kings Cross and get on a train to York to meet a man there. You'll know him because he'll be a Chinese gentleman and there aren't that many in York, see. He'll find you if you wait at the exit. When you give him your package, he'll give *you* a package and you need to get back on the train to London just as soon as you can. Remember, whatever you do don't look inside the bag at any time. Very dangerous chemicals. You mustn't talk to anyone about this, even your parents. It's top secret. We don't want any other *paint companies* to know, do we?'

'Yes, sir. Kings Cross. York. Chink. Package and back to London. I didn't know the paint business was so exciting, Mr Snipe.'

'I know, son, if only they knew, eh,' Snipe said, ruffling the boy's curly hair.

'Hush will fill you in with all the details after our meeting. Did you like your soup, mate?'

The boy nodded and there was a gentle knock at the door and Theodore Hush entered.

'All ready, Mr Snipe. I'll brief the boy now?'

'Yes, and get Jim while you're at it.'

Down in the factory, Tom heard Hush shouting someone's name over the stairs. His manager jumped to attention and had a look on his face that Tom couldn't describe. It was a sort of combination of fear and sadness. Even though he was never friendly to Tom, he felt sorry for the man as he turned and slowly walked up the metal steps, looking down at his feet as he went.

He looked to some men drinking their tea and joking with each other and saw something he hadn't noticed before. In between each machine he could see a cloth sack with metal pipes poking out of them.

Over in Chelsea, a leech began to awaken. Two more wriggled, slowly coming to life. As they crawled up their glasses, the bell began to gently tinkle. Some left behind were still sleeping, curled up at the bottom of their glass prisons.

The Night Shift

Back at the factory, all the boys sat quietly as Tom read out the words from his book. The two brothers Lefty and Righty huddled together. Righty had no left arm and Lefty had no right. No one really new why. They were a good team though. Curly sat on his stomach propping his head up with his hands on his chin. The tall skinny boy who everyone called Sticks, sat with his back against the wall looking like a tree trunk snapped in half, his long legs stretching outwards.

Lichtenberg Figures are created by painting the surface of the wood with a conductive solution of sodium bicarbonate and then applying 10,000 volts of electricity across the now partially conductive surface. As the high voltage electricity is discharged through the insulating wood, the electric field causes a physical breakdown of the bonds between the atoms in the insulator, creating a conductive path for free electrons to flow. The flowing current heats the wood and causes it to burn.

Curly raised his hand.

'Does that mean electricity can be controlled on any surface?'

'Very good, Curly, it does, to an extent. However, the surface must be partly conducive to burning. Like wood in this case. If we turn to the chapter on Electric Willow the Whisp, we can see how lightning can be attracted by holes and vents in the ground and that...'

'Break time is over!' Jon shouted as he burst into the area under the stairs, tapping the metal staircase with a spanner and ringing his bell.

'Before your afternoon shifts, we've got important news to announce. Good news. Mr Snipe has won a new contract so there's a big order coming in. The bad news is you lot have to work an extra shift tonight.'

'We need to go home, Jon, it's unfair. You didn't tell us before today,' Righty said, raising his good arm.

'Yes, Mr Snipe never told us about this,' Lefty chimed in.

'Never you mind what Mr Snipe says. You're talking to me now and these are his orders. You'll be getting an extra wage for this week anyway, so don't complain.'

'Where we supposed to sleep, Jon?' Sticks asked.

'There's blankets under the stairs, with room enough for all of you. You'll be getting fed tonight too. Those who have parents, make sure you tell them today and be back here by six. Now get back to your shift.'

That afternoon, his shift ended, Tom picked his bag up and walked to the door as always, but this time jumped over to the right behind one of the last machines in line. He poked his head around to see if anyone could see him, then moved with his back to the wall to the storage cupboard. Inside the dark space, Tom covered his nose as he leaned against the mops and buckets. After some time, he listened for the last man to leave and the door slamming. The factory was silent except for the distant thunder.

In the stillness of the factory, Tom searched for the metal pipes he had spotted earlier. As his eyes adjusted to the darkness, the big machines slowly appeared on either side of him in blocks of grey.

A lightning flash revealed a pipe in one of the gaps between two machines. He bent down and pulled. It was heavier that he thought it would be and tried to use his body weight to lift the object up. He soon realised it was connecting two machines, fastened in place.

Walking further up the machine corridor, he turned to his right and another object caught his eye. He could just make out a sack cloth at the base of the extruder with an object poking out of the end. He bent down to feel his way. Inside he could feel hard objects of various size and shape. Leaning back, he dragged the bag free. Then pulled the pieces out, their metal scrape echoing along the hall.

He could just about see the bag containing pipes of different shapes and lengths. He chose a long straight one and a short curved one, they made a dull metallic thud as he rummaged around. He realised that if he put them in the right position, he could connect them together with a twist and a click, the paint oozing onto his hands as he did so. Also, inside the sack were a pair of vulcanised gloves and eye protectors. He held them up in the brief lightning flashes to inspect them.

Wearing the gloves that went all the way to his elbows and eye protectors covering most of his face, he edged up the metal staircase, the bag clanking behind him with each step. The thunder was beginning to smash down on the factory above and rain was pelting on the glass roof of the back of the factory. The horses were becoming agitated, fidgeting their hooves in the gravel.

Stopping at the top landing, he could see a large office through an ajar door and pressed on to its right, following to where the sound of the rain seemed to be louder. At the end of the hall there was a stepladder and he could see a small square window with a hatch in the ceiling above it. Climbing up, he pushed but the door wouldn't open so using his head he managed to heave the hinged door open, rainwater pouring in on his face like a captain on a weather-tossed ship.

He pulled himself up onto the roof, dragging the bag up with him. He looked around, squinting through the rain and saw two chimney stacks with a gap between them. He emptied the sack onto the roof and climbed up and lifted the pipes up to them. With some effort he managed to wedge them perfectly between the two structures, with the long pipe facing up to the sky and the curved section pointing out at a right angle to the opposite rooftop.

The storm was right over Shoreditch now and sparks appeared and disappeared up and above his head. One came down and seemed to turn towards him, making him jump down to get out of the way.

As he watched, a single ball of light shot down near the pipe, falling onto the water-soaked roof with a hiss. He jumped up, adjusted the vertical pipe and stepped down, turning his head with one eye closed, to check the angle.

The next ball dropped, turned and entered the pipe and extinguished in a fizz of spray. Tom covered his mouth and held his head, trying to contain himself as he stepped back, almost slipping over, away from the chimney behind the roof hatch.

Then a fatter globe came spinning down and clattered through the pipe, shot out of the bend and flew across to the other roof, just missing a pigeon that flapped away in a splash of loose feathers and water.

It was soon joined by others of varying sizes, as they descended, spat out onto the roof one after the other like giant fireflies. Tom laughed to the heavens, sparks of light reflecting in his eye protectors, his fists shaking above his head.

Five Lads

It always starts the same.

Night shadows stretching across floor and ceiling. A humming. Full of sound but also soundless. A sustained deep note.

The dog staring directly at him. One eye shining blue. Pleading.

Jumping down from the privy into the silent corridor, feet sinking into the soft oriental patterned carpet.

Feet keep sinking. The more he tries to move, the lower he sinks.

The surface of the carpet is now at waist height. Its pattern, with red and green streaks moving as he tries to stay afloat. If he stands still, the pattern flexes back into shape and he sinks lower. The feeling is heavy, like wading through thick woollen treacle, as he strains to reach the other end of the corridor.

It always ends the same.

Just as he is sinking lower, a soft gloved hand pulls him up and out onto the bookshop floor, he is shivering and covered in colourful threads of oil and woolly fabric. He feels a blanket around him. Warm and comforting.

'Baxter, wake up!' Jon shouted.

Tom's hand knocked over the tin water cup as he jumped out of the tangle of blankets on the floor and hit his head on the metal staircase.

'Well done, lads, we got it all out last night.'

In came Curly, edging to the understairs area as if that part of the room was in some way safer.

'Alright, Curly,' they all said.

'Sticks, Tom, Lefty, Righty,' he replied.

The keys in the lock of the front warehouse door jangled. Arthur Snipe entered, speaking with someone who was in the street and just leaving.

''Ackney. Yes, 'Ackney with an *hache* like 'addock, 'alitosis and 'enley fuckin' Regatta. You got that? Now fuck off.'

Today, Arthur Snipe was in an unusually good mood.

'Hello, my boys!'

'Morning, Mr Snipe,' they answered tiredly.

'We did it. Our biggest order ever. A record. Out the door in less than ten hours. *Snipe's paint covers the Albert Hall interior.*'

He gestured with his hands to an invisible sign above his head.

'Wallup! That's a bit of fucking history that is. Tomorrow, we celebrate. It's a party and everyone's invited. Even you lot. Jon, make sure all the food is stocked upstairs. Get the beer and gin. A lot. And what's that bloke with his piano?'

'Bert,' Jon says.

'Yes, Bert and his bird. Whatsername, the one with the big tits. Annie or Ally?'

'Alice,' Jon corrects.

'Of course, yes. Bert and Alice.'

'Will do, Mr Snipe.'

'Tell them to put the piano down here and have them arrive by eight o'clock. Invite all the chinks too, as well as the other workers and their wives if they like. Also get some birds from Hoxton for the lads. Classy ones, mind. No expense spared. We'll have a right knees up! Now clear off, no work for the rest of today!'

The boys chatted excitedly. Tom stretched his shoulders, said goodbye to the others and walked towards the front door.

'Not you, Tom.'

All the boys stopped and turned.

'You lot piss off. Just him.'

Tom nodded for them to leave.

'Yes, Mr Snipe. What is it?'

Snipe made sure all the others had left before speaking. He started to pace around in small circles. He seemed to be deep in thought as he caressed Lady's handle. He stopped pacing and turned to look down at Tom, who was partly hidden by the metal staircase.

'What are you *up* to, Tom?'

'What you mean, *up to*, Mr Snipe?'

'I found something the other night after work. Something that seems... how do I put this? Out of place.'

He pulled an object from behind his back. Tom's mouth went dry like paper.

'What exactly is this?'

'Oh, that, it's a book, Mr Snipe.' Tom said relieved.

'I know it's a *book*, Tom. What I mean is, what d'you want with it? You work in a factory not a fucking library. You can't read.'

'I can. I like readin'. I like readin' that book. It's mine.'

'Oh, it's *yours*, is it? What's it about?'

'Science an' that.'

'Looks boring to me. Not enough pictures for my liking. I'm more of a *picture* person when it comes to reading,' he said, skimming through its pages.

He dangled the book in front of Tom like a worm on a rod. Tom tried to grab it but missed and fell, Snipe laughed as he did so.

'It's my book give it to me. *Please*. Please, Mr Snipe.'

'Oh well, seeing as you said *please*, you can keep it.'

He repeated the same game and Tom fell again, much to Snipe's amusement.

'Oh, dear! Catchy, catchy!'

Snipe threw the book to the floor, the pages fluttering open. Tom reached for it and just as he pulled, Snipe pressed his boot down on it, Tom ripping a page out and falling backwards.

'Whoopsie daisy. Tell you what, you can keep that page and I'll keep the rest. How's that?'

As Snipe scraped the book towards him along the gritty floor, Tom edged back to his bedding, hugging the crumpled page to his chest.

'I enjoyed that. Games are so fun aren't they, Master Tom? Now you can fuck off. I'll see you at the party and whatever you do, don't take any books with you.'

Snipe walked up the metal staircase to his office carrying the book with him.

Tom carefully unfolded the page, looking up to Snipe's office and back to it, a tear forming in his eye as he smoothed it over. It was then that he noticed, and in fact remembered, something important about that particular part of the book. He read the page carefully once more. One solitary tear dropped onto the page then he opened his eyes again with clarity.

The Tempest Prognosticator

Over in Chelsea, the Tempest Prognosticator started to vibrate. One leech began to slowly wriggle.

It twisted and turned and strained up its glass wall. When it reached the top, as if to encourage the others, it shook its head slowly from side to side, looking down to the remaining glasses.

In their glass beds, the other leeches began to stir and come to life, twisting, stretching and feeling their way. They began slithering up. Their bodies spreading out against the round edges of the glasses with each effort of movement.

As two more ascended and reached the top, the bells started to chime gently, then all of the shiny black creatures crawled together. All as a team. All as one.

A small crack appeared at the top of the cylinder, travelling down its length to form a fissure. The cylinder cracked open releasing a dark stench of earth and rotten moss.

Now the leeches were screaming as they moved beyond their confines, growing in size, pulsating, oozing black out of the shattered opening as the hammers smashed the bell again and again.

Mum

As he walked into number nine, Tom peered into their room to see if anyone was home. Three men he had never seen before were sat talking quietly with his dad. Opened beer bottles covered the table. Tom looked around the room. His dad stood.

'Hello, son. I didn't expect you back so soon.'

'No work today, Dad. Where's Mum? Where's Mary?' Tom said craning his neck around the room.

'Gone.'

'What d'you mean gone, Dad. Where's all her matches?'

'She's not doing that anymore, Tom. She's working at a different place now.'

'What d'you mean?'

'Never you mind, Tom. Just let me see these gentlemen to the door and I'll explain.'

'What's happened, Dad?'

Frank Baxter led the men out into the hall. Tom could hear them talking carefully under their breath. When Frank Baxter returned, his tone suddenly softened.

'Look. It's just you and me now. She'll be back soon, don't you worry. Now make some tea and I'll explain.'

Tom reached up to the stove, lit the fire and placed the teapot out on the table with the cups. He looked over at his dad who was calm and controlled. Not his usual emotional way.

'You know your mum loves you, Tom. She loves all of us.'

He paused and ran his hands through his greasy hair.

'Thing is, it's not good for her to be here.'

'What do you mean, Dad?'

'It's my fault, son. It's all my fault. She's gone to live in another house. Somewhere she can look after your sister.'

The kettle whistled loudly, interrupting the conversation, the water bubbled and frothed.

'Where, Dad? What house? *Whose house*?'

'Well, it's a sort of house where there's all women and they look after each other, see. It's not far, it's in Mare Street, so you can visit her any time. Let's have some tea, eh? I don't know 'bout you but I'm well parched.'

With both hands, Tom heaved the kettle down, and poured the water into the giant chipped teapot, the steam filling the room and burning his forehead. In silence they sat, not really knowing how to continue talking.

'How's your job, Tom? The paint place? I'm sorry I was so hard on you, mate. I'm still proud of ya.'

He reached to touch Tom's hair, but the boy pulled his head away and took a sip from his tea without a smile.

'Job's alright. The owner's a right wanker though.'

'Language, Tom!' Just because your mum's not here it doesn't mean we can lower our standards,' his dad said half laughing.

Another long silence.

'Where's the house, Dad?'

'You can go any time. Just say who you are and they'll let you in.'

Frank pressed one meaty palm down on the stained newspaper on the table, tore off a corner and wrote the address on the scrap.

195 Mare Street Hackney

'Here, Tom. You can go after tea if you like,' his dad said in a cheery voice making it sound as if he was giving Tom permission.

'She went cos of you, didn't she?' Tom said looking to the floor.

'Now, Tom, don't be like that. Everything's going to be alright from now on.'

Tom ignored him and silently finished his tea, jumped down from his chair and placed the cups and teapot in the sink without a sound.

He turned to his dad for the last time.

'Goodbye, Dad.'

'Say hello to your mum from me. I'll make some tea for you when you get...'

But he had already slammed the door to their room.

Tom walked out of number nine and nodded to Old Joe. Before heading up to Mare Street, there was one more visit he needed to make.

It was then that he noticed a scraping, swishing sound further up the street.

When he arrived at the Roper's, he saw Greg Roper sweeping water and hay off the pavement to the road.

Tom ran to the window.

'Sorry, Tom,' Greg just said, shaking his head as he continued to brush away at the muddy pavement.

Tom felt the open window frame with its chipped edges, looking around the empty space that now seemed huge. Even though it was cleaner than it had ever been, Tom could still smell her through the hay. He saw a crushed carrot top scuffed into the floor.

'It wasn't me. One night she just sat down and that was it. I swear to you,' Greg said.

Tom reached over the window and picked up the carrot top, blew the dust off it and placed it in his pocket.

Over in Mare Street, Tom read the words above the door. It said: Elizabeth Frey Refuge for Women. Tom opened the front gate and stepped up to a wide paved path with rose bushes either side. Women tended to them as they carried bags of earth this way and that. Some of the women noticed Tom and talked behind their hands as he walked to the grand doorway.

He pressed the large white door button, and a faint tinkle could be heard from within, as he removed his cap and smoothed his hair down. Behind him, the women in the rose garden were craning their necks and giggling in a group.

A matron with a white habit and severe spectacles answered the door. The women scattered back to work in silence.

'Yes?' was all she said as she looked past Tom and back down to him.

'I'm Anne's son, Tom.'

'Who?'

'Tom Baxter, I'm Anne Baxter's son.'

'Ah, so you are,' she looked him up and down and smiled. 'Come in, young man.'

Inside was a wide stone hall and a front desk to the right in a small alcove. Behind it, the nuns were busily working away at all sorts of ledgers and paperwork in an office. Some looked up at Tom smiling.

The matron moved round to the desk and opened a great big book. The cover flopped back with a thud and she moved a bony finger down a list of names.

'B, B, B... ah, Baxter. Anne. Here we are. Straight up the stairs. Through the hall. Turn left. Room 104,' her voice echoed around the large empty hall.

Tom looked at the two sweeping staircases either side of the huge crucifix hanging from the ceiling and didn't know which one to take. He turned back to the matron.

'Either of them will do. At the top take the corridor.' the matron pointed with a flicker of a smile.

Tom looked at all the paintings on the walls as he ascended. Jesus Christ and shepherds with their flocks mainly. Each one had a gold frame and they were of varying sizes, placed in a higgledy-piggledy sort of way. The one that caught his eye was that of a well-dressed man atop a beautiful brown horse. A grand house was in the background and a river flowed in front of him as the clouds floated by. As he looked, he felt the carrot top in his pocket.

At the landing he could hear voices along the corridor. Women's voices. Some whispering. Some shouting. Some laughing, but not many.

As he reached 104, he raised his hand to knock but the door opened.

'Tom, my love!'

Anne pulled him up, swinging his legs from side to side. His mother smothered him with kisses. Her breath was strong with liquor.

'Mum, what you doin' here?'

As Tom pulled away, he saw her face. One side of her cheek was brown, like the colour of an old peach. She turned her head to the window.

'They look after ya. They are good people really, Tom. I've even been learning gardening. They try to get us work too.'

The white, empty room had a small crucifix above the bed. A large window overlooked fruit trees and gardens. You could see the nuns busily carrying apple baskets and folding white linen into neat piles. Some sang as they worked. Tom sat on her bed and his mother sat close to him in silence.

'Was it Dad?'

'What, Tom?'

'You know what I mean.'

She moved her hand up to her face.

'Look, Tom, your dad's a good man, it's not his fault. He had some bad luck that's all.'

The following silence resolved nothing.

'Anyway, how are you, Tom? How's the job at the paint place, eh?'

'S'allright, s'pose. Got a party. Celebration. I've got a… friend too. I'm meetin' her by the canal tomorrow.'

'Look at you. All grown up with a girlfriend. Job an' all. I'm so proud of you Tom.'

'So how long are you here, Mum?'

'As long as it takes to get back on my feet. Maybe a few months.'

'A few months? What about my sister?'

'She's with my mum in Manchester, she'll be coming here soon. Then we'll all be back together again. You'll see.'

Tom looked to the floor.

'But what do *I* do, Mum? I mean about Dad. I want to stay here with you.'

She took both of Tom's hands in hers.

'Oh Tom. I'm sorry, it's not allowed for you to stay here. Against the rules. Look. *You* need to look after *him* now,' she said, pointing to his chest.

'Just until me and Mary get back. You're in charge. Just try and control his drink and he'll be better. You have to do that, Tom. Can you do it for me at least? I know the way you feel but it's the only way for now.'

Tom lowered his head as he swung his legs from side to side.

'S'pose so, Mum.'

'Oh, I almost forgot. I've got something for you. Here.'

She turned to a cabinet by the window and opened a drawer, retrieved a small object and passed it to her son.

It was a tiny book of common prayer and it fitted perfectly in the palm of Tom's hand. He touched the cover and opened it carefully. In the front was a pressed lavender flower, its faint perfume was still present.

'I know you like readin'. I can't read very well anyway,' she half laughed.

'Thanks, Mum. I like the flower too.'

'It grew just here in the garden. Can you read some to me, Tom? I'd like that.'

Tom opened the first page and began. She had never heard Tom read before and couldn't quite believe how good he had become. Anne Baxter closed her eyes as Tom's gentle voice filled the small room. The rhythm of the words like a balm over her forehead. Each line sounded like a musical instrument, like the notes of a guitar or a violin. Notes of words. Sounds and pauses of a musical composition.

A gentle knock broke the trance and Anne opened the door to one of the nuns.

'Gardening time, Anne. We're pruning the roses at the back today.'

'Thank you, matron. Tom, I've got to go.'

She gave him a big squeeze.

'Enjoy your party and remember you can visit any time you like.'

'I will, Mum.'

'Look after your dad. Remember what I said.'

They both walked down the staircase of paintings and Tom let himself out into the front garden and looked back, but his mum had already gone.

The Canal Warehouse

The following morning Tom waited at the canal bridge, looking at the market traders beginning to pack up for the day. Clouds like giant ship sails slowly expanded across the sky.

As he turned to the top of Goldsmiths Row, he saw her. Vanessa was riding one of those new cycling machines. Everyone stared at her as she came rattling up the gentle slope towards him without a care in the world.

'You came all the way on that?'

'Good lord, Tom, no. A friend in Clerkenwell lent it to me. What do you think?'

'Is it 'ard. I mean, don't you fall over?'

'Not at all. Look.'

Vanessa dismounted and bent down.

'See these things. They are called pedals. They attach to this chain. All you do is move them round. You just have to make sure you go fast enough so it's stable. Look, it's easy.'

She got back onto the machine and skilfully turned in a circle, attracting a crowd of passers-by.

'Can I try?' Tom asked.

'Only if you're careful.'

'We can go this way, look, along the canal. It's where I want to take you.' Tom pointed.

Tom mounted the machine and wobbled before taking off down the cobbled slope like a racehorse, Vanessa chasing after him, Tom shouting, his voice rising and falling with the bumps in the road. As they reached the bottom of the hill, the gasometer loomed over them.

'So, what do you think, Vanessa?'

'I love it, Tom. There's one in Battersea but I've never seen one this close.'

'I knew you'd like it. It's for storing gas. When the works are full, the sides pull up like a curtain.'

He raised his hands together to demonstrate.

'Look, I've found a way we can see it from above, follow me!'

Tom gestured towards some warehouse buildings where men were lifting bags off the wooden platform dangling from the window. Each time a bag was dropped, the smashing noise echoed across the water as the men shouted up to each other.

Tom proudly ushered Vanessa ahead of him as if it were the entrance to a grand hotel.

''Ere, upstairs.'

'Will the cycle be safe, Tom?'

'Don't worry. Put it inside.'

Vanessa leant it against the wall and they both went running up, their footsteps echoing through the stone stairwell. Inside, the temperature was cooler and the smell of sweet grain surrounded them. Up and up they went, the steps becoming steeper, the ceiling lower. When they reached the top, Tom opened both arms wide to reveal a wall of windows overlooking the canal. Each piece of glass was a small square held with dark lead in a criss-cross grid.

Up here the sun gave the room a fog of orange dust. Looking down, the gasometer was now a round space, its white centre gently rising from the ground like the crown of a giant goose egg. The canal boats looked like toys and the people like mice. Dots moving along veins and arteries leading to the black snake of the canal.

'I love it, Tom,' Vanessa said staring down.

'I brought you something too,' Tom said slightly nervously.

Vanessa turned, the edges of her hair luminous red, framed by the light of the windows. Tom was holding a fresh white rose in paper out to her, its whiteness contrasting with her shadowed face.

'How beautiful, Tom. Thank you.'

She took the flower and held it up to her nose and placed it in her hair, then kissed Tom on the lips. Tom's heart flapped as he embraced her.

'You planned everything perfectly, Tom,' she whispered in his ear.

'I did, and yer know what?'

'What, Tom?'

'I've another plan. It's goin' to happen down there. I want to thank you, Vanessa. Thank you for all the 'elp you've given me these past months. I don't know what I would've done without yer really.'

'I don't understand, Tom. Whatever are you talking about?'

But he didn't answer, he just gazed down to the gasworks. One half of his face was in shade, the other bone-white to the window. On his cheek the blue paint stain seemed darker than before, his eyes matching that darkness.

Down at the gasometer he could see it flutter black in the wind, a raven waiting for the right moment perhaps. But the waiting was now over. The storm was coming.

October 2022

Simon

The Hackney Resident wasn't exactly his first choice. Years ago, Simon Beaver had visions of an illustrious career. International correspondent for a broadsheet or investigative journalist for *The Atlantic* perhaps. It was never to be. Still, at least he could walk to work, and even though he had an 'editor' he was his own man. To a point.

It was a doddle really, which allowed him to do side-gigs blogging for restaurants or well-paid English tutoring on company time. They didn't even care. Most of the stories he had to cover were people whinging about the Clean Air Zone or the lack of bins. He was lucky to be gainfully employed. Mid 40s, paunch, still being paid to write. It was a lot more than could be said for most of his peers who were twice divorced, alcoholics, heart attacks. Bitter memories of past glory days. The slow lane it was, but at least it was his lane. This morning he was lucky to be investigating a story right on his doorstep.

Shoreditch's Boundary Estate was a unique London neighbourhood. Orange-brick mansion blocks fanned out from a raised circular park — Arnold Circus — with a bandstand at its centre. The wide, tree-lined avenues gave it a faint cosmopolitan air, completely incongruous to some of its neighbouring streets that still existed from the late 1800s like Old Nichol Street and Chance Street.

Peering past the tall trees and foliage of the park, Simon could just about spot the blue and white tape flapping and hear the digital squawk of police radios. A small crowd had already gathered, and coppers were gently pushing the onlookers back from the scene.

Simon edged through the crowd showing his press card to the others in charge.

DCI Amanda Saha made eye contact and motioned for him to move to the side, away from her colleagues.

'Another gang stabbing?' Simon asked.

'I thought I asked you to come later.'

'Good morning to you too, Amanda. I couldn't help myself and anyway, it's in my manor. Sorry.'

'He had drugs on him but they think cause of death was something else,' Amanda answered.

Something else?

'And another thing. He's covered in brick dust.'

'Brick dust?'

'Yup, you heard me. Brick dust. Covered in it, like a giant Dorito.

'There's something else...'

'You keep saying that. Yes?'

'Simon, you know we have our little arrangement. Back-scratching and that. Well, I need a bit of a favour on this one. I can't tell you anything more for now, it's a bit... Can you keep this under your hat for a while just until we get things straight? We've got the elections coming up, you know how it is.'

'What am I supposed to write then?'

'Just the usual. Gangs, which is true, drugs blah blah. I don't know, you're the writer.'

'Amanda, I'm not a writer, I'm a *journalist*, there *is* a difference.'

'Oh, the *mighty* Simon Beaver, Pulitzer Prize winner of bin articles and park barbecue complaints.'

'That was a low blow.'

'Simon, I'm sorry. Look. Full contact at every point of this thing but just keep it you know, *stabby*, if you know what I mean.'

'Stabby?'

'Yeah, stabby. Just for a while. I promise.'

'What else aren't you telling me?'

'Sorry, Simon, that's all I can say for now. Oh, and don't mention the brick dust, you didn't hear that from me. Right.'

Simon shook his head and wrote some notes on his phone and then looked around and wrote some more.

'You know I hate this, don't you?'

'I know, Simon. I promise, I'll sort it and it will be all yours.'

As the evening drew in, a plastic bag floated away to wherever homeless bags floated away to. Simon walked the final steps to Shiplake House on the estate, clicked the keypad and entered, the door slamming with an echo as he ascended to his fourth-floor flat.

At his front door, his cat also called Simon, mewed a hello and rubbed around his ankles as human Simon picked up the post on the floor and entered his kitchen. The rounded American-style fridge was empty except for three bottles of Carib and a takeaway tray. He grabbed a beer, twisted it open and sat down at his dining table/Zoom desk/breakfast table/living room ornament.

He got a message on his phone via his tutoring app:

Hi I saw your details they looked good. My son needs help with his reading and 11+ can you start this weekend? I'm in South East London.

Simon sucked back a swig of beer as he accepted the gig and sat to open his post. To some, teaching was a calling. To him, that calling was from his bank account. It wasn't that he didn't care about the job. Far from it. He had a good reputation. His students had passed exams, got into top universities and schools up and down the country. All good. But it wasn't exactly a passion. Being a journalist for a local rag didn't come with a high-flying salary and the tutoring wasn't stressful. Win win as far as he was concerned.

The flat was cool and calm. In the glass reflection of his Citizen Kane poster, you could just make out the edges of the trees in Arnold Circus and see the lights of each flat gradually go on as the late summer darkness slowly descended.

Greenwich

The following morning at Greenwich Peninsula, Simon stepped out of the Uber and looked up the wide pristine intersection. All the buildings were covered in scaffolding for new cladding to be added. The green membrane of plastic giving the building a distorted shimmer.

As he was early, he took a nose around to kill some time. At the end of the scaffolding-clad avenue he could see the opening of where the Thames met open sky. The road ended at a seaside promenade of sorts, with smart residential townhouses facing the river. He put on his sunglasses as white static fizzed on the water and looked across to the Thames barrier, over to the bobbing boats and then down to the muddy beach. Half-submerged bicycle wheels and ancient bottles, all shining black as if crafted from one sculptural mass.

He got a text.

I'm downstairs.

Simon walked back to where the taxi dropped him and saw a small man in shorts waving at the base of the scaffolding, his long mono-beard blowing sideways away from the Thames.

'Hi, Simon, is it?' the dad asked with a faint Australian accent.

'Yes, you contacted me about your son's English lessons.'

'That's right. Come far?'

'No, just Shoreditch.'

'This way.'

The bearded man led him to the brand-new glass entrance and keyed in the code with a buzz.

'They all look the same because of the scaffolding,' Simon said.

'The whole thing has been an expensive shit show.'

'I can imagine.'

They ascended silently in the immaculate lift and came to the sixth floor with a gentle jolt. The dad jumped out of the lift and turned right along plush soundless carpeting. Simon had to lurch to keep up with him.

They reached number 609 and he pushed open the door to a chaotic living room of books, cleaning equipment and piles of washing. His oriental wife said hello as they entered. She was picking up toys and books from the floor and placing them in a bright red plastic basket like a farmer at harvest time.

'Right, this is Robert. Say hello to your new tutor — Simon.'

'Hello, Simon.'

Robert extended his little hand in a formal handshake and Simon shook it with a smile.

'How old are you, Robert?'

'Eleven and three quarters. Birthday's in September.'

'That old, eh?'

'Now, as I outlined in the email, he needs help with his reading comprehension. Here are the books he's used so far. Now, sit down, Robert, and make sure you do what Simon tells you.'

'Yes, Dad. Simon, have you seen my comics? I've got a Spiderman one and a Hulk one — look.'

'Robert, Simon's not here about your comics.'

'Don't worry, I like comics,' Simon answered, smiling to him.

'Okay, I'll leave you to it. Coffee's over there and there's a water bottle on the table. We'll just be next door.'

The bearded dad and his wife skipped into an adjacent room and closed the door.

'So, Robert, have you heard of Life of Pi?'

'Is it about pies?'

'No, it's even better, it's about a *tiger*. I'd like you to read the first chapter about where the main character — a boy — comes from.'

Robert started to read slowly and Simon listened carefully.

'*My suff-er-ing left me sad and gloomy*... is this a sad book, Simon?'

'*Kind of*... in parts. But it's also full of *excitement*. You wait.'

A giggling could be heard in the next-door room, followed by a slapping sound.

Robert turned round distracted.

'Okay, that was very good, Robert, now read the next bit.'

'Aca-demic study and the steady, mindful practice of religion slowly brou... brought me back to life.'

More giggling, followed by panting and moaning.

Now Simon turned around.

Robert looked at him and raised his eyes, sarcastically.

A line of brightly coloured pictures of dinosaurs and mountains started to bang on this side of the wall with each thrust. Reaching a crescendo, the last picture in the line fell to the floor with a crash.

The dad came bursting out of the room, dressing gown fluttering behind him, beard and hair at odd angles.

'Is everything okay? I heard a noise.'

'*The picture*, Dad.'

Robert pointed behind him, keeping his eyes on the book.

'Oh, right, no problem, we'll tidy that up later, hey,' said the dad.

He disappeared into the bedroom again.

'So, Robert, would you like to continue?'

'I have kept up what some people would con-sider my strange relig-ious prac-tices... does the tiger go to church, Simon?'

'No, this is the boy, remember?'

'Oh yeah, sorry.'

'After one year of hi... high school...'

The moaning began again, followed by a rhythmic screaming, then the pictures started to shake once more.

An hour later, the class finished and the dad, red faced entered the room.

'All done?'

'Yes, all done,' Simon said as he looked to the floor.

'How did he do?'

'Really well. It's a challenge, Life of Pi.'

'Is that the one about the magic pizza?'

'No, the tiger.'

'Oh, yeah, we saw the film. How was it, Robo?'

'Noisy, Dad.' He pointed to the bedroom door.

'Now he's got mindfulness class and *shooting*, haven't you, Robo?'

'In that order, I hope,' Simon said.

'Thanks, Simon, I'll see you same time next week?'

'Yes, that works for me.'

On the way out, Simon avoided shaking the dad's hand.

As the taxi whisked him home to Shoreditch, the landscape slowly altered. North Greenwich, with its futuristic towers and high-end flats slipped away to reveal old London. Victorian terraces, dark brick and narrow streets, the odd park dotted about. Moving around London this fast sometimes felt like being in a time machine. A time-lapse flicker book going forward, flip the book round and move back in time again.

Sunday Night, Monday Morning

As the ten o'clock news murmured away in the corner, Simon brushed his teeth and got an SMS. He picked up his phone and continued brushing as he checked the message, dots of toothpaste foam spraying the screen.

Hi I saw your profile it looks really good. Are you free to help with my dissertation on Zoom?

Simon quickly accepted the lesson and pressed send.

He flopped into bed and started to read a few chapters of his book. Beyond his window, the hissing sound of the trees in Arnold Circus was comforting.

As he sat down at his laptop, the Zoom call made its customary ping and he opened his note pad, pen at the ready.

When the image appeared on the screen, instead of the usual window onto someone else's private life, he could see a green field with a low wooden fence. In the distance a wooded area could just be seen and the sound of birdsong filled his earbuds. A cuckoo called to the right and the sun bounced yellow-orange flares over from the left.

As a bumble bee hummed noisily into the frame, a horse walked into view. Not really a full-sized horse but more of a donkey. Its thick tufted ears flicked as the bumble bee flew around its head. Simon looked down and realised he was still in his check pyjamas. His pen began to bend and elongate, curl like a black earthworm.

As he spoke, the only sound he could make was a neighing combined with a distorted video-call sound. As he tried again, a deep throated braying came from his mouth. The donkey on the screen froze and unfroze with digital static. The animal nodded and snorted as it got closer to the fence. It seemed to be smiling.

Simon looked down and the pen was stretching, twisting and curling round his hand. It slithered up around his wrist and wound around his forearm.

Morning light in a bedroom haze. The deep hum of a trapped bee could be heard by the window. Its size magnified by the distortion of the curtains. There was a notification on his phone. Simon yawned, scratching his head, propping himself against the pillows as he squinted at the screen. The message was from DCI Saha.

As he shuffled over to the kitchen and placed the pod in the coffee machine, he recited in his mind exactly how he was going to write the gang murder article. Mysterious circumstances (maybe), gang-related (check), a possible stabbing (obviously), investigations are ongoing, blah blah blah. He sat on the toilet and tapped a rough draft into his phone before his shower.

The only upside about today was that Amanda was now ready to share any information she had. She was good like that. Although she annoyed the fuck out of him, he respected her. One of youngest female DCIs in that part of London. However, it did mean she was super cautious. She didn't like risks and knew full well that she had to play by the book more than her peers. Most of the time she would keep him on the inside track and he would have to walk the line between journalistic integrity and not being too alarmist; it was a case of writing an interesting story whilst making it generic enough for it not to go national.

Lucky for Amanda, Simon was utterly unambitious and addicted to gossip. The best kind of gossip, the kind that wasn't allowed to be divulged whatsoever. Of course there were some minor indiscretions in private company around the dinner table, but he was always careful. It worked for both of them, but Simon definitely got the shit end of the stick.

Anyway, his job would be done by AI before too long. Did anyone really care about real journalism anymore?

He looked at himself in the mirror, checked his teeth and smoothed down the collar on his jacket. Even though he had already reached the boring sweater phase of his life, he still cared about his appearance.

This morning, Amanda offered to meet him near his house before work. She tried to make it seem that it was *her* compromise but he knew full well she needed the article out fast; she would dish, and he would give her a rough edit of the article on his phone. Gossip for him, peace of mind for her.

He walked around Arnold Circus and turned onto Calvert Avenue with its sudden downtown Manhattan vibe, past the Community Laundrette displaying its patchwork window of thank you letters. A Vietnamese girl with spikey hair and pink flip flops was scraping gang graffiti off the entrance to her new boutique. The next week it would reappear, the day after that, she would be there wiping away once again.

Looking at his messages, he noticed that the previous night's lesson request was from someone called Dorris and it had been deleted for some reason.

'Oh, you're in civies, almost didn't recognise you,' Simon said quietly as he sat down opposite Amanda on an outside café table. The benches looked like striped Brighton rock glistening in the morning sun.

'Very funny. What you got?'

'*No* morning how are you? Just straight for the main course. You are harsh DCI Saha.'

He slid the phone over to her. She scanned it quickly.

'Fine.'

She slid it back.

'Coffee?' she asked.

'No thanks, just had one,' he said, stretching.

'Well?' Simon asked.

'Well, what?'

'The *something else*. Remember?'

'Oh, right, yes.'

She pretended to forget.

'It seems the victim was electrocuted.'

'God. Like an accident?'

'Well, obviously.'

'But it's a gang murder.'

'No, *correction*. You are writing that it's a gang stabbing. Remember?'

Amanda lowered her voice and came closer to him. He noticed her full lips framing her perfect teeth as she spoke.

'Look. He was electrocuted, yes. But place of death was right there too. He wasn't taken from a train track or a garage. Nothing like that. There were no bare wires near him. Not even a substation nearby. Most of his teeth were completely melted and we've got no fingerprints because his arms were basically burnt off. Happy now?'

'Well, well, well. That *is* something.'

'Yes, it certainly fucking is. We've got a team onto it. Modded tasers. Car batteries. You name it. It's a right fucking pain to be honest. I've got a shit load of other stuff to get through.'

'Mum's the word, *ma'am*,' Simon said, tapping his nose.

'What about the brick dust?'

'Right, they're still doing tests but the body was full of it. Mouth. Nostrils. You get the picture. Maybe a result of the electrocution?'

'Creepy.'

'Indeed. Very. Couldn't have happened to a nicer bloke though. He used to run county lines gangs down to Cornwall and Bristol. He was also a nonce. Real family man.'

'Can I include that?'

'No, not yet, please.'

'Name?'

'Sorry, Simon.'

'It's going to be a very short article.'

'You're good at those, remember?'

Amanda checked her phone and got up to leave.

'Is that it?'

'Yup. I'll keep you posted, Simon. *If* I feel like it,' she winked and walked down the road.

Simon watched her as she walked further up to the corner and got into an unmarked car. It pulled out and melted into the sea of traffic going up Shoreditch High Street.

He was left with a hollow feeling in the pit of his stomach. Another Monday; he stood and headed for his offices in Hackney.

Even though he was on foot, he was moving faster than the traffic going up Hackney Road. While he walked, he thought about the electrocution. Maybe it was a new form of gang retribution: a signature, leaving a sign; something like that. As he slowed at the canal at Broadway Market, he googled *electrocution gangs London* and bookmarked the results, making his way to the south end of Mare Street past all the new eateries and bars that had popped up in recent years.

Some street traders were working even though it was a weekday. The morning office crowd were here to get a taste of bohemian heaven. Even if it was in the form of a twelve quid Ciabatta.

As Simon headed north to Hackney, the sun dipped behind a clump of clouds and the road shadowed. Next to a rack of second-hand sportswear, the green parka slipped off the rail and the tracksuit trousers with it. A pair of white vintage sunglasses came down off the display and the items disappeared underneath a food stall.

Adeolo

Over in Poplar, Adeolo was playing Fortnite on his PlayStation on the 50-inch screen that dwarfed the sitting room. On the screen two brightly coloured characters climbed over rooftops shooting down at the enemy. His best friend was playing with him remotely and they recorded it on their YouTube channel, Adeolo making comments through his headset as they progressed through the game. The sounds of the loading and re-loading of Adeolo's gun and his mum's frying pan filled the small flat.

'Adeolo, time to stop now, dinner's ready,' his mum called through from the kitchen.

Adeolo lowered his shoulders, paused the game and said goodbye to his friend, typing something in the keyboard that made them both laugh.

As he paused the game, he noticed a movement at the window. Something that never happened because they were on the third floor. He jumped down from his gaming chair and stood on the sofa by the window and pulled back the curtain fully.

He saw a movement in the waving branches of the tree outside the window. A shape of a person. A piece of shiny green. A flash of white. Then it disappeared.

'Come on, you,' his mum said as she placed the fish and rice on the table.

Adeolo just stayed at the window with his back to his mum.

'I thought you were playing your game. What are you looking out there for?'

'Thought I saw something.'

He jumped down and sat at the table.

'You funny thing,' she rubbed Adeolo's hair.

Just when she sat down to eat, there was a knock on the front door. Adeolo's mum put down her cutlery with a sigh.

'What now?' she said under her breath.

She opened the door to a tall broad-shouldered man. Black cap and hoodie.

'Hey,' she said looking to the floor.

'Sorry, is this not a good time?'

'No, no, don't worry. Come in. I was just making some dinner. Would you like some?'

'No, I'm good. I just wanted to see how Adeolo was doing,' he said, craning his neck.

'Of course. Come in.'

The minute he entered the room, Adeolo ran towards him.

'Hey, big man,' the visitor said.

'I got to the next level. Look,' Adeolo showed him the score on the screen.

'He's not interested, Adeolo.'

'No, I don't mind. Show me. You're gonna be a pro someday,' he winked at Adeolo's mum.

They ate silently and after a while they cleared the plates together to take them to the kitchen.

'Can I play my game now, Mum?'

'Alright, just half an hour then bed.'

He jumped down and rolled the TV out again.

In the kitchen, she washed the plates as he dried.

'Listen. Any news about his dad since the accident?' he said.

'The bastards didn't renew his licence. Can you believe it? It was only one eye. He's been driving for them for five years. No compensation. Nothing. Just like that. It's not been easy since it happened. He's gone off the rails a bit. We're having a break. Adeolo sees him on weekends now.'

'What are you doing now his dad's not working?'

'I'm selling that Herbal Living in the estate and online. Social media.'

'You know everything'll be fine.' He placed his hand down to hers. She pulled away slowly.

'I know. Thanks. We really appreciate your visits. Adeolo really likes you.'

'I'll pop round on the weekend to see how he's doing. See you, big man,' he shouted over to the living room. Adeolo shouted back.

He left, closing the door quietly behind him.

Adeolo's mum leaned her back against the door and breathed in. She looked at the time on her phone and shouted through to her son.

'Right. Adeolo, get ready. Bedtime. Put your stuff away now.'

He paused the game and pushed the TV back, jumped up to the sofa and took one last look out of the window.

The Hackney Resident

Hackney had experienced a gentrification pincer movement since Simon had worked in the area. Existing prosperity from the west was breaching the bulwark of Kingsland Road, while hipster Shoreditch was spreading up from the south. New cafes and shops, like brightly coloured coral growing on old rock had started to cluster along Mare Street's southern end, spreading northwards, slowly displacing the weak and underfunded in its wake. Shoreditchification was truly underway.

In contrast, the small lane right up at the north end — formerly the Narrow Way — still displayed some of the poverty once seen in the whole borough. It sometimes felt like the south end of Mare Street had been tipped up, and all the vulnerable, unlucky and feckless had rolled down into it. Smackeys rubbed shoulders with crackheads and old Jamaican men, as the world they once knew transformed around them.

As Simon strolled further north into Clapton, the streets gradually became dirtier. Chicken boxes and chip wrappers floated like confetti on top of black skid marks of archaeological chewing gum. Half-squashed beer cans rolled around tunelessly, clattering like a music hall piano played to an empty audience.

The Hackney Resident occupied two floors of an old 1980s tile factory, ironically named Innovation House. The window frames were peeling with aggressive red paint. The open plan office sat at ground-level and the newspaper shared the space with a start-up that sold fashionable pet accessories online called *Je ne Regrette Chien*. Every day, boxes of the stuff were piled in the hall, blocking the door to the newspaper's main entrance.

Jill, the receptionist/runner/junior writer greeted him with unbearable cheerfulness as he entered.

'Hey! Simon.'

'Yup,' he simply replied.

She had recently declared herself gender neutral and asked everyone to include non-gender pronouns under their emails. Somehow this seemed to be more important to her than an actual land war happening in Europe that could tip over into nuclear Armageddon at any moment.

Some staff members had already started adding their own pronouns like 'hat' and 'biscuit'.

Simon slipped into the kitchenette. There were two types of coffee in the world. Shit coffee and good coffee. Simon liked both. He reached up to the cupboard and pulled out the jar of shit coffee and shovelled a spoonful into his cup as the kettle boiled. While he waited, he leaned against the fridge and looked back to the tutoring app. Dorris's profile had simply disappeared. The kettle filled the area with moist bellowing clouds and he poured the water into his cup, creating a dark slurry of a drink. He sipped at it as he made his way over to the goldfish bowl for the Monday morning meeting.

Inside, the editorial team and art department gathered around the central table. Through yawns and coughs, everyone exchanged stories of weekend escapades, drinking adventures, family get-togethers and barbecues.

'How was your weekend, Simon?' Jill asked enthusiastically.

'Oh, the usual, you know.'

The Zoom call with the donkey came back to him. Less a memory, more a feeling. Small details surfaced. Simon's heart rate quickened. His eyes dilated and he began to sweat.

'You alright, Simon, you look a bit peaky?'

'Yeah, Jill, I'm fine thanks, love.'

The Editor in Chief, David Abara, smoothed down his close-cropped goatee and began the proceedings. He always started the meeting with the same three words and a secret betting system was in place in the event of him not saying those three words. It had happened on a couple of occasions, so the odds were good. There was already over five hundred quid in the pot.

'Right, yes, good.'

Two staff fists bumped. Another group held their heads in their hands.

David looked up at them briefly, confused.

'Nice to see you all bright eyed and bushy tailed. So, the agenda for today is as follows. Carol is on the statue story by the town hall.'

'Cool. I've already done a few interviews and a local poet has offered a piece to the newspaper,' Carol said.

'Sounds good. Michael can follow up the fox thing. Apparently, another was found by the Lido, so ask around. Also, the carnival piece needs to be with me by four.'

'Sure,' Michael said.

'Simon, what are you on?'

'I've already conducted some interviews with a contact in the Met about a gang murder in the Boundary Estate, I'll have a first draft over to you this afternoon?'

Simon had already written a second draft and proofread it.

'Good stuff. Another thing has come up. Apparently someone has been crapping in pizza boxes and leaving them in front of people's front doors again.'

A silence followed. Everyone started to look at their phones.

'Can I do it?' everyone turned to Jill, her hand held up, eyes wide with excitement.

'What would we do without you, Jill? I'll get you started and you can investigate it, how's that? Now if there's no other business, let's get to work, people.'

Everyone stood to the sound of scraping chairs and notepads closing. This was Simon's chance to get back to his desk for a catch-up on Twitter, and to write a *Time Out* review of an Edwardian themed Asian restaurant called *Chicky Chicky Bang Bang*.

At 3 p.m. on the dot, he sent in the article to David. After a few minutes, he got back some minor feedback. Simon quickly amended it and mailed it back. By 4:03 he had turned off his computer and slipped out of the office.

He walked back through Hackney Central and onto Mare Street, past the chicken shops, phone accessory shops, chicken shops and phone accessory shops.

Since when had chicken become so bloody popular anyway?

As he walked past CashCreators he saw a boy wearing a green parka look through the window, hesitate and then enter just as an ambulance tore past.

A New Neighbour

That evening was a rare golden-orange. The low autumn sun lurked behind Arnold Circus, twisting fingers of tree shadows across the pale wooden floor of Simon's flat. He was on his second beer and enjoying an album a friend had recommended. The first song blasted from his old Denon sound system and out of the open windows as he padded about the flat.

He heard a banging from above and turned the volume slightly lower. As the violins of the next track began, he heard the banging again.

He lifted the arm on the turntable and listened. It sounded like someone moving boxes. A sort of scraping and humping.

He had got to know the owner over the years before they moved overseas and the flat had been empty for a while.

The other residents kept to themselves and at times it was a little isolating. Good to have someone new in the building.

As he was about to lower the needle back on the record, there was a gentle knock at the door. Simon walked over, pulled the bolt across and opened up. A tall attractive woman in a vintage dress with bare feet was standing there looking flustered.

'Sorry about the banging. I just moved in.'

'Oh, not a problem. I thought it was me. The music.'

'Oh, Lord no. I love music. Was it violins?'

'Yes, well the beginning was.'

'I like violins,' she said.

'Sorry, would you like to come in?'

'No, no. Too much to do. You know. Upstairs,' she said as she pointed upwards.

'If you need anything, feel free to call round,' Simon said.

'What do you mean?'

'I've got a tool box. I mean, if you need. You know *tools*,' Simon moved his wrist with a twisty motion.

'Oh, yes, of course, will do. You didn't tell me your name,' she said smiling.

'Simon. And yours?'

'I'm Nena.'

'Righto, Nena. Welcome to Arnold Circus.'

'Welcome to *where*?'

'*Here*. Arnold Circus. That's what it's called sometimes. Well officially, Arnold Circus is the park within the estate. But you get the idea.'

'Of course it is. I'm miles away, me. Sorry, Simon, it's all the moving.'

'Yeah, it can be stressful. Anyway, feel free to drop by anytime.'

'Will do, Simon. Thank you.'

He closed his door and walked into the kitchen, got out a bag of pasta and put the water on to boil. He opened the fridge and heard the scraping and humping upstairs once more, as he reached up to a saucepan from above the hob.

Simon the cat, who had been lurking around the fridge, suddenly flicked his ears and darted to the living room.

The cat started making strange grumbling, bubbling noises from under the sofa.

As Simon walked over to turn up the volume, the green cupboard handles blinked and opened like eyes.

The cupboard eyes looked left and right and then followed Simon around the room. They squinted, half closed as if focussing on something in particular. As he turned to go back to the kitchen, they blinked once more, closed fully, and then transformed back into their original form.

Simon the cat jumped up onto the kitchen top and hissed.

'Oi, greedy, you've already had yours.'

Simon prepared the rest of his meal and then sat down, the steam rising into what was left of the sunshine pouring into the living room windows. He peered down at his phone as he slurped the pasta and took sips of his crisp cold beer. The orange sun dimmed to a dark brown and then to black as the evening slipped by.

There was a knock at the door.

It was Nena standing in the doorway. Vintage dress but a different colour this time. She was also wearing strange formal shoes and a floral scent of some kind.

'Off out somewhere?' Simon asked.

She just stood there smiling shyly. Then she gently approached him, reaching over, as if to kiss his cheek. But instead, she spoke. The sound was close, more inside his head than inside his ear. The gentlest of whispers, a pleading request.

'See that he gets it. Will you do that for me, Simon?' she said.

A gust of wind slammed the door shut, echoing down the stairwell.

Poplar

It was midday; thirty-five degrees even though it was autumn.

Because it was Sunday, Simon had decided to take the scenic route by bus. He was beginning to regret that decision.

The airless 277 smashed over the potholes past Victoria Park on its way south to Mile End. Passengers were fanning themselves, sweating where they sat. Fussing with their smartphones, wrestling with stroppy children.

The bus stopped just beyond the park and a stocky old man dressed in a thick woollen blazer and check woollen cap got on. His ebony skin had a dry patina but his eyes were bright and wise. Somehow, not one part of him seemed to be sweating. Simon recognised the old Rock Against Racism T-shirt under his jacket.

As the bus jerked away, he staggered to the back near Simon where the free seats were. He had a jaunty way of walking with his elbows in the air.

Every now and again the man would let out a gentle laugh, as if he was in on a private joke. No one else seemed to notice this. Simon turned away to the window.

After a few yards, the man pressed the bell. When his stop came, he giggled one last time, winked at Simon and left.

Simon slightly embarrassed, reflexively checked his watch and looked around to see if anyone else had seen what happened. They hadn't.

When Simon turned to look at the bus stop, the old man was gone. He looked up and down the street, but there was no sign of him. No one seemed to notice this but him. He looked around once again. Everyone was just busying themselves with their kids or scrolling on their phones.

Simon shook his head lightly and pulled out *his* phone to comfort himself. He looked up from it and let out a sigh. *What the fuck just happened? Maybe the guy had just crossed the street, or ducked into another road. He was pretty spritely. Yes, that was it. He must've just legged it.*

Satisfied but still a bit unnerved, he looked back to Google Maps on his phone. The route was going to be quicker than he thought. The lesson request had come from a mother near Canary Wharf. This area wasn't familiar to him and he was looking forward to visiting a new part of London.

He looked past the driver and through the windscreen as the glassy stone towers of Canary wharf reared up, the river and the City of London in the distance.

The bus stop that ran through Canary Wharf Station was shaded from the boiling heat. A short walk took him to the bright, open vista of West India Quay with its posh eateries sitting on the water. Small round BBQ boats like floating hot tubs milled about, their occupants passing drinks and listening to music. A breeze blew up, cooling the sweat on Simon's back and he breathed in the clean air.

According to the map, turning right took him to Poplar Station, to where the motorway brutally divided old from new. The metal structures of the station and the construction for the new train line turned the air to darkness once more: subterranean.

It wasn't easy to find, but you could just about see the lift to the walkway that took you over the motorway. He took the lift to the first floor and stepped across the glass hamster tube that bridged the two worlds, the lift descended on the other side.

In the estate's car park, surrounded by blocks of brown bricks and maroon paint, Bangladeshi children chased each other with buckets of water and super-soakers. One of them squirted a jet of water at Simon, catching him right on his shirt. He pretended to be angry and raised both hands like a monster, the kids squealed and ran off.

Simon texted the student's mother.

Think I'm here
Not sure where to find u
She replied.
Don't worry I'll come down

Simon saw a woman waving from a walkway in one of the buildings and he made his way up the steps to the door.

It was cool and dark inside the flat with a narrow hallway that led to a sitting room. In the middle of the room, a little desk with two chairs facing each other had been set up. The only light came from the window, partially covered by a ripped curtain.

'Kids got you,' she said pointing to his wet shirt, laughing.

'Yes, they did.'

'I'll get you a towel. This is Adeolo.'

A boy with a red Minecraft T-shirt was standing awkwardly at the desk.

'Hi, Adeolo.'

'Hi,' he said looking to the floor.

'Would you like a drink of anything, tea?' the mum asked.

'Just water, thanks. It's hot out there today.'

'I know, tell me about it.'

Simon placed his leather backpack on the floor and removed his books. The room felt like the middle of a tornado with its contents flung out to the edges, out of the way. A huge TV was pushed against one wall. Chairs and a digital piano were stacked by another. Maybe a party had taken place the night before.

The mum returned with a large glass of water. Simon took a sip. It tasted of meat fat and washing up liquid. He put the glass to one side.

'So, what's he been doing so far?' Simon asked.

'He's doing his exam in six months. I've been using this.'

She handed Simon a test book.

'Okay, I've got something to start him off with on reading comprehension based on the same kinds of tests. Let's start with that. Then we might get on to some writing. Sounds good, Adeolo?'

'Sounds good,' Adeolo said.

As the boy read, Simon looked around the room and breathed in the air. It had a faint smoky smell. Aromatic but stale. When Adeolo finished, Simon asked him a few comprehension questions.

'Now a bit of spelling.'

'I hate spelling,' Adeolo said.

'Tell me about it, so do I. You know I can't even spell the word *hat*.'

Adeolo laughed.

Simon made a sad face and looked down.

'What, you're serious?' Adeolo said.

'Yup. Look. T-H. No that's not it. A-T... oh, I give up really.' The boy laughed again.

'H-A-T. It's easy. Simon, are you a real teacher?'

'I'm not sure, Adeolo.'

After 45 minutes, his mother who was working next door, entered the room.

'How's he doing?'

'Very good. He got most of the comprehension questions right but he needs to work on his handwriting and spelling. His reading and lexical resource is really quite good for his age.'

'Well done, mate, you bossed it.'

Simon held his hand out to shake the boy's hand. A broad smile crossed his face as he shook. Before Simon left, he asked to use the bathroom.

'It's just through there. But be careful the seat is a bit...' his mum said.

He entered the cramped cubicle and carefully lifted the seat which would only stay up if you held it in place. Inside the bowl, a huge skid mark of shit greeted him and an overfed fly buzzed out. Simon kept his mouth closed. There was hardly enough room for both of them in the small room.

He carefully placed the seat down again and flushed with his hand covered in a scrap of toilet paper.

'Is there somewhere I can wash my hands?'

'Just through there.'

Simon scrubbed away and dried his hands on a manky looking towel on the rail.

'This isn't our usual place. It's temporary you know. We only just moved here. It's a bit... complicated.'

'I see. Well, I'm off. I've given him some writing homework and I can look at that next time. How does that sound?'

'Would the same time next week be good?' she asked.

'Oh, yes, I'll have to check my schedule but should be okay. See you.'

They both came to the door and Adeolo waved happily saying, 'Goodbye, Simon, see you next week!'

Simon stepped out of the estate, removed his antiseptic gel bottle from his bag and squeezed out a big dollop. Pity. *Nice boy. They'd find another tutor in no time. He was sure of it.* As he walked, he deleted Adeolo's future lessons and checked a tutoring notification from a student based in Knightsbridge and accepted it immediately.

It was now around six o'clock and the light was being swallowed up fast. He entered the lift to the walkway and pressed the first-floor button, it moved slowly up. As he exited, he squinted along the glass-topped hamster tube and saw that someone was holding the lift door open for him. He could just make out the woollen jacket; it was the old man from the bus. Simon quickly walked through the hamster tube so as not to keep the man waiting.

When he arrived, the lift door was closed. He pressed the button impatiently and it opened, revealing an empty space.

He looked down to the stairwell and caught the man's woollen cap turning at the bottom of the stairs, his black hand holding the rail.

Tom ran down after him, two steps at a time. He jumped to the corner at the bottom almost knocking over a mother with her pram.

'Careful, mate.'

'Sorry. Sorry.'

She rolled away tutting at him.

Simon ran his hands through his wet hair, breathing heavily. A deafening motorbike engine jolted his heart.

He turned towards Canary Wharf. He was almost running as he took each step as if it would be somehow safer at the station.

Out of breath, he made it to the bus stop. As it was a Sunday, the road was quiet. Despite the heat, the covered area felt dark and claustrophobic. The odd passenger came out of the glass doors from Canary Wharf Station, trolley bags in tow but other than that, the whole street was deserted.

On the bus the lower floor was empty and a pleasant breeze blew in from the open slits of the windows. He sat down and exhaled then closed his eyes as his body temperature dropped and his heart rate lowered. The humdrum whirr of the motor and the squeak of the glass windows as the vehicle flexed and bounced along was comforting.

Then he could feel the woollen jacket lightly scratching his bare arm. There was an unusual burnt smell like singed hair.

Simon kept his eyes tightly shut, his mouth turning to cotton wool.

Then he heard the voice, deep but soft.

'Simon. *Simon.* Open your eyes.'

His heartbeat was going through the top of his head. His bowels turned to ice.

The man was sitting right there next to him. His dry skin like black sand. Creases around his eyes, deep and pitted. He flicked his fingers over his cap in a sort of greeting or salute.

'Listen, Simon. The boy. Adeolo. Keep an eye on him. You have to. If you don't, he'll get into shit. Do you understand?'

'I... I Promise. Yes,' he said, even though he had no idea what the old man was talking about.

The man winked once more and Simon closed his eyes his heart rate thumping through his chest and temples. His neck was cold with sweat.

Simon opened his eyes slowly and he once again had the whole bus to himself. It jolted to a stop somewhere near Mile End and a family got on, one of the kids banging the hand rail as they scuffled upstairs.

The Maiden

Simon jumped off the 277 and hurried up Mare Street to the Maiden. It wasn't his usual watering hole but this was an emergency.

'Jameson's. Double. No ice please.'

The modern, cavernous space was more cruise ship canteen than pub. Swirly carpets, that could accommodate all shades of eventual vomit, paired with faux-Victoriana. A plastic horse brass here, a steam engine print there. It was a strangely comforting distraction from the events from earlier. Simon was good at compartmentalising his emotions. Distracting himself. If something wasn't in his control, that was someone else's problem. The whisky also helped.

'Here you go,' the barman said.

Simon took a good sip.

Near the bar underneath a framed picture of an old fireplace, two men sat opposite each other. One was talking aggressively but quietly. The other, his head lowered, body language of a scolded puppy. Simon could just about hear them.

'So, how many we got so far?' the man asked the other, jerking his head up to him.

'Six boys in total, a couple from Hackney, three from Clapton and maybe another.'

'So, that's one thing you didn't fuck up. It's coming in tonight. Heathrow. Make sure they know where they is going. The food goes up with the boys. The paper comes down with dem. Nice an' easy. Tell the first lad to go to Bristol to plug the gap left by Kenny, who is fuck knows where...'

Simon zeroed in on the conversation more closely.

The waitress brought food to their table. The man waited for her to leave before continuing.

'I *knew* there was something not right about him. You introduced him, Max. You fix it, got it? Find out where he is and bring him to me ASAP.'

'Hunter. I'll sort it, bruv, don't worry.'

Simon pretended to sip his glass that was already empty and swivelled his stool round to try to listen more closely. The chair squeaked loudly as he did so.

Hunter looked around.

Simon squeaked his chair back again so he was facing the bar.

'Max, if this isn't sorted, you're dead, bruv,' he slammed his hand on the table.

A security guard carefully stepped close to their table.

'Is there a problem, gents?'

'Nah. All good.' Hunter winked.

As the pub began to slowly fill up, Simon stepped down from the bar stool and without looking back, slipped out of the pub as quickly as he could.

Ling's

Hunter got into his Mercedes E Class. Slipped into the traffic on Mare Street and headed to Bow. Like most business owners,

Hunter had cashflow problems. But for him, this meant doing drop-offs in a few trusted bars, clubs and restaurants up and down the city. He could eat and drink for free seven days a week if he wanted to. That JDs was making a right killing from the sports bags.

Because of that mug Kenny, tonight he had to make a drop himself. He cruised up to Victoria Park humming to a Tankz track, puffing vape smoke out of the open windows.

Ling's was opposite Tesco Express on Bow Road.

He pulled into a side road and looked in his rear-view mirror. Jumped to the boot, pulled out the sports bag and walked back onto the main road to the restaurant.

Ginger and garlic hit him the minute he entered. Narrow dining room, small red lanterns dotted on either side. The atmosphere hot and humid. The place was pretty quiet except for the sound of clanging woks coming from the kitchen.

He caught the eye of the manager who pointed for him to go to the back. He was led to a side door with a combination lock. Inside, Kim Ling who was on the phone winked as he raised a Chivas bottle with two glasses. The desk was a mess of papers, files and collapsing in-trays. Ling was speaking Mandarin. He covered the phone with his hand and apologised silently to Hunter and ushered for him to sit.

He finally ended the call.

'Sorry, Hunter. Uncle in Beijing. Got bollock cancer. Drink?'

'Yeah, why not.'

Ling poured out two generous measures and passed him the glass.

'Here's to not getting bollock cancer!'

'I'll drink to that,' Hunter said.

They clinked glasses.

'Listen, Kim. Next time, it won't be Kenny. I had to get rid of him.'

'Oh, dear. Sorry. It happen. HR alway problem.'

'I'll send a picture before next time, of the new guy.'

'Sure. Listen. Hunter?'

'Yes, Kim?'

'Twelve per cent, right?'

Hunter stopped mid-sip.

'Twelve per cent! You havin' a fuckin' laugh? We agreed ten.'

'Inflation, Hunter. It not my fault.'

'What, you're fucking Barclays Bank now?'

Ling tapped the edge of his glass and looked around his office, lips pursed like a fat toad.

He let out a manic laugh, as if the punchline of a joke had just been delivered.

'Heeeeyyyyyy.'

Ling pointed an arthritic finger at Hunter.

'I got you. Got you good, mate.'

Ling noticed Hunter wasn't laughing.

'Listen. I got special tonight. Fried oysters. You wanna try? Real good. Fresh.'

'No, I'm good, Kim. I'll be in touch.'

Hunter swigged the rest of his drink, pushed the sports bag under Ling's desk and left.

As his Merc pulled back onto Bow Road, a blue moped edged out and followed at a distance.

Southbank

Hunter glided into his basement parking space, clicked the lock and headed to the lift. On the twelfth floor he got out and entered the hall onto plush carpet. Instant smell of industrial cleaning; bubblegum and BO. It had the pressurized, soundless atmosphere of a recording booth. You had the feeling that anything could happen in these halls and no one would ever know about it. He walked left and opened the door to his flat.

The spacious living room was empty except for a TV on one wall, a gym treadmill and a white sofa. Grey. White. Black. Not too much deco. The only colour came from the large painting on the wall behind the sofa. It was a life-size portrait of Henry VIII but instead of the king's face, it was Hunter's. Well realistic. A mate gave it to him. An in-joke from back in the day when Hunter used to sell puff to his mates. On the pager, they used to call a *Henry* an eighth of weed. Maybe still do. That's where he started. Now look at him. King of Bankside. King of E9. King of N1. King of the fucking lot, mate.

The room had a wrap-around balcony with floor to ceiling glass. He looked out through the multi-coloured rain dots across the City of London. In the reflection, his face merged with the flood-lit view of St Paul's Cathedral, the dome a pointed skull, the columns an oversized grin. He looked east to all the little flats with their little people. *Lights off. Tucked up in bed before Monday morning. Tube – Office – Home – Repeat. Mugs.*

Down in the street, Simon Beaver sat on his moped, idle exhaust fumes mingling with the red brake light. He looked up to the window, pinned the address on Google Maps and texted Amanda.

got something you might be interested in re. electrocution
UR welcome
Simon

Amanda

As Simon watched her enter the café, cold morning air entered with her, making the hanging planters tremble on the terracotta wall. Light jazz played in the background to the grinding of the coffee machine.

Even though he wanted something from *her* this time, Simon couldn't help feeling a certain frisson. Did he really want to *please* her?

He sat smiling with his arms crossed as Amanda walked towards him, this time in full police uniform.

'Why here?' she just said, looking around the space.

'Oh, you know, thought it might be a bit more interesting. Spice things up a bit.'

'Okay, what you got, Simon? I've got a ceremony to attend.'

'Hence the uniform, I suppose. Actually, Amanda, I was going to ask you the same question.'

'What do you mean?'

'I know his name.'

'Who's name?'

'Mr *Dorito*,' Simon said under his breath, hand to the side of his mouth.

'How?'

'I've been doing some digging of my own,' he crossed his arms and smiled some more.

'Go on.'

'But first, I need something from you.'

'Alright, what, Simon? I'm not going for a drink with you, if that's what this is about.'

'Don't flatter yourself. Although, that's quite a good idea actually. Maybe another time. Anyway no, I need you to do a records search. Someone who died a while ago. Can you do it?'

'Maybe. When you say a while ago... who is it?'

Simon fidgeted in his seat.

'Okay. He's, I mean *was* about 70 years old. African male. About 5 foot 6. Strong looking. He likes, *I mean liked*, to wear flat caps.'

'Oh, well, that narrows it down.'

'Year of death was in the '80s sometime, I would say.'

'Okay, that's only a few million. This is going well.'

'There was something about him.'

Amanda looked up.

'When? What do you mean, Simon? You knew this person?'

'No. I don't know. Just try it. I've got a feeling.'

'None of what you're saying makes any sense. You know the search will be flagged up. I'll need an officer and it'll be logged.'

'You can say it's part of *Kenny,* the Dorito guy.'

'So, that's his name? Okay, so, how do you know?'

'He has a very unpleasant boss.'

'Name?'

'Amanda, I need that search, please?'

She looked to the ceiling of the café and then breathed out.

Simon noticed her slender neck muscles. The way they tensed up as she stretched.

'Look. Tell you what, I'll give you my database password. You've got it for 24 hours only. That's it. It's the best I can do. Only, *and I mean only,* use it in the evening. They monitor everything. I'm serious, Simon, this could get me in a load of shit.'

'I promise. Evening only.'

She slid over her phone with a screenshot of the password and Simon took a photo.

'Thank you, thank you, Amanda, this is really...'

'So, who is it?'

'Hunter someone,' Simon replied.

'Hunter Paris?'

'I don't know. He was with someone in the Maiden pub called Max who looked quite scared.'

'Hunter Paris. Fuck.'

'What, Amanda. Did I do something wrong?'

'No. No this is good. But, Simon, stay out of this from now on. I mean it. These people are... Also, it's complicated. Part of something ongoing.'

'Money laundering?'

'Simon, what aren't you telling me?'

'Nothing, I promise. I just guessed. Everyone knows these people rinse their dosh in this way.'

'What, you're fucking Ted Hastings now?'

'Ted *who*?'

'Never mind.'

Simon considered his next words carefully. He wasn't sure if he should tell her but blurted them out anyway.

'I followed him.'

'For fuck sake, Simon. When?'

'Last night.'

'How.'

'On my bike. I was careful. He went to a restaurant. Some Chinese place.'

He looked down to his phone and showed her the photos of the licence plate.

'Ling's in Bow.'

'Fucking hell, Simon. I'm telling you stay out of this, it's not safe. I'll have to involve the law if you don't.'

Some of the other customers were looking up to their table. Simon lowered his voice.

'But you *are* the law, Amanda,' he said with a frown.

'Look. Simon. I'm telling you. Stick to your job. I'll stick to mine. This really isn't for you. Please?'

There was a lilt in the way she delivered that last word. He suddenly saw her eyes change. Soften. Just for the briefest of seconds.

Just Call Me Erol

The next day at work, Simon sat at his desk all day and ignored his co-workers even more than usual. He checked his tutoring app. None for now. The time was 3:03. That was too early to leave even by his standards. He drummed his fingers on his desk. *When Amanda said evening, what exactly did that mean? After six? Ten? Midnight? Well, it certainly wasn't three in the afternoon.*

Simon got a tap on his shoulder from David.

'Got a moment?'

'Sure.'

Simon entered his office. David closed his door which was something he never did.

'All good, Simon?'

'Yeah, why?'

'Look. I'll get straight to it. Do you like your job? I mean working here at this paper.'

Simon tried to answer but was cut off.

'Thing is, we've noticed you slacking off a bit. Now don't get me wrong, you're a good worker. You meet your deadlines. You write well. Investigations par excellence. It's just that we could do with a bit more *oomph*.'

'Oomph?'

'Yeah, you know. *Love*.'

'Love?'

'Yes, for the job. Over at the Gazette they covered the murder you were on and they found another angle. Something more interesting. Look.'

David flopped the paper over and Simon saw the headline.

'County lines gangs? How odd. I heard it was just the usual gang bollocks,' Simon said.

'Well, you heard the wrong bollocks. The Gazette's all over it like a hot rash. It got to the Standard. But the Gazette broke it. Even before it went online. What happened, Simon? My star reporter get gazumped this time. Surely not?'

David softly punched his arm.

Simon coughed, looking to the floor.

'Sorry, David. Won't happen again. I'll check my sources more carefully next time.'

'Don't worry, Simon. We just need a bit more...'

'Oomph,' Simon completed the sentence with a light movement of his fist that accidentally seemed sarcastic.

'You got it,' David replied.

'Oh, Simon, can you get Jill in for me? I've got something for her.'

'Anything I should be doing...?'

David laughed.

'Simon, we're all good. Look, don't worry. Just more love and stop leaving so fucking early it sets a bad example for the others.'

'Righto, David.'

For the rest of the day, Simon completed all his expenses, which bearing in mind were three months late; it kept him busy until ten past five. When he left, he made sure David saw him.

As he walked down the Narrow Way, he saw George as always. His sales patter had become three syllables through repetition. *Can you spare some change, guv?* was now the rhythmic mantra of *sparechaingu, sparechaingu, sparechaingu.* Everyone was now efficient. Even George. Simon popped a one pound coin into a dust-worn clammy hand as he slipped past Hackney Central Station.

Simon fretted as he turned the corner.

First the horse incident, now seeing people on buses. Maybe I should call a doctor? Granny had dementia but this seemed different. Less a deterioration more of a sudden affliction. It couldn't be that surely.

Remember. The. Super. Power. Ignore something for long enough, it usually went away. It didn't do to dwell on things. If you did, they just grew beyond one's control. Metastasised. Even if that small grain of something was nothing, it would soon become something given half a chance.

He reached his building in record time and almost breathed in the biggest daddy longlegs he'd ever seen in his life. He swatted it away and it floated past the bathtub planters under the window.

Up in his flat, he went straight to the fridge, opened a beer and sat at the dining room table. Simon the cat was sleeping over on the sofa, the street lamp clicked on and picked out his white whiskers as he sullenly opened his eyes and looked over to Simon with a look of pure disdain.

Opening his laptop, he fired up his web browser, checked his phone and typed in the URL. A black screen greeted him with the user name password fields and he entered the details Amanda had given him.

A white screen popped up with a search field in the centre. On the left various tick boxes ran down the length of the page to refine the search.

Simon typed in the man's description, estimated age and year of death.

A page of blue faces scrolled up and down on Simon's glasses.

He refined the year to 1979. The year of the Rock Against Racism concert in Victoria Park. Again, a page of faces looked out at him but fewer this time.

A faint burning smell entered the room. Not strong but just noticeable.

Simon ignored it.

He looked down the list of refinements and saw that you could filter by cause of death. He inputted the word *electrocution* and hit enter.

'Hello, Simon.'

Simon jumped up and looked behind himself. The man from the bus was sitting in the chair by the window. His legs were crossed and he was holding a steaming cup of tea as if he'd been there all along.

'Who the fuck are you? Get out of my house or I'll call the police.'

He held his phone up.

'Now, now, Simon. That shouldn't be necessary. Look. Sit down and let me explain.'

Simon just froze. Still standing. One leg lightly shaking.

'Please, Simon. Give me a chance and I promise I'll be out of your way. Sit. *Please*,' he gestured with his hand.

Simon sat obediently, his knee bouncing up and down.

The man breathed out dryly.

'I'll cut to the chase. I've been sent by someone. *A fraternity.* It's a little hard to explain but suffice to say we need your help.'

He had a way of enunciating his S's.

'Are you... you know. Dead?' Simon asked.

'Yes, I'm afraid so. Well correction. I *was* dead. By the way, good detective work. You were spot on. I suppose it was the T-shirt that gave it away. That concert was quite a day, yes. *Steel Pulse* stole the show. Unfortunately, I had an accident on the way back. Got on the wrong side of a rail track.'

He raised both hands and made an electrical sizzling sound through his teeth and laughed.

'Never mind about all that. I'm here about Adeolo.'

'Yes, my student. What about him?'

'Shouldn't that be *ex-student*?' Erol said with his eyebrows raised.

'Well, I can't take on *everyone*, can I?'

'No, but you have to continue with him. He's in danger and you can help him.'

'What sort of danger? By the way, who the fuck are you? If I'm going to have to talk to a ghost in my own home, I need to know their bloody name. It's a rule I have.'

'Just call me Erol, Simon. You need to do two things. Firstly, you need to keep his teaching going. If he falls behind, there's drugs, the lifestyle.'

'How do you know about the boy?'

'It doesn't matter how I know, Simon. Second, and this is most important point. You need to contact Tom so he can help you. Or rather you need to help him contact you.'

'Tom. Who the fuck's Tom. Is he another tutor?'

'Not really. You'll know him when you meet him. The book will help you.'

'What book?'

Cash Creators

Bright red logo over the whole shop front. DJ decks, smartphones and musical instruments crowding the window. Everyone knew CashCreators sold moody gear.

As the buzzer rang, Max dropped his fried chicken on the counter, wiped his hands down his trousers and pressed the security button to unlock the door. The deafening sound of an ambulance siren blasted into the shop from Mare Street. A boy entered.

'Excuse me, sir. Do you sell moth balls?' the boy asked, green parka hood over his head, white-rimmed sunglasses.

'Wot?' Max said.

'Moth balls, I can't seem to find em, sir.'

'You havin' a laugh? This is CashCreators, not John Lewis.'

'John Lewis? Where can I find this *Mr Lewis*?'

'Westfield.'

'Which field? Is it that near the Weavers Fields?'

'*Stratford*, mate. You know, the shopping centre,' he said, pointing behind him as he filled his mouth with chicken.

'Shopping centre...?' he said under his breath.

The boy looked around the strange shop. Floating ice cabinets of shiny black objects marked with symbols, strings of black hardened oil dangling off them below a sign saying PS4 £100!!! Flat metal boxes with circular plates in them. Sculpted guitars made of lacquered wood, brass instruments and small pianos of glossy hardened oil. A huge black box was against one wall with colourful lamps that flashed red and green. Repetitive, pounding music seemed to be coming from it like a marching band of hammers and clanging bells. Somehow, though, there was no orchestra to be seen.

Safe in the knowledge that there were in fact no moth balls, he left the shop silently. Max kept a close eye on him as he did.

Outside, the sky was a crystal blue, the sun bright. Yet he felt no warmth from it.

The street was familiar and yet so unfamiliar. On the pavement, ladies with umbrellas and gentlemen with top hats merged with the *other* people. These were of many nationalities and wore strange under-clothes with writing on them. They all held small, black, rectangular objects over their ears and talked into them as if afflicted by a madness. Most simply stared into them as if hypnotised by their own gaze.

Everyone seemed to be rushing about this way and that. Talking and shouting all at once. Together yet alone.

Carriages travelled in one direction, as small four-wheeled horseless carriages smashed in the other. It was like watching a shiny glass dividing the two; objects travelling left, the others directly right.

People looked down from the windows of big red horseless omnibus. Images and shapes smashing together and sending out multi-coloured diagonal lines in their wake.

He wondered if everyone could see in this way.

He began to recognise where he was. The odd building stood out, not many but just fragments to navigate by. Familiar brick walls like pieces in a jigsaw. He realised he was walking south down Mare Street which meant that the house would be just down on the right.

His legs moved faster as he got closer. Past the church on the left and further along where crumbling shops met giant green windows.

Along the length of the area that should have been where the house was, a shiny wall of some sort stood. It had writing all over it. The boy read.

Lux-ury flats com-ing soon — buy your-self a p... piece of Hackney his-tory.

The writing was next to a symbol of some kind that featured a picture of a house and a tree.

He crouched down and peeked into a tiny gap at the base of the wall. The large front yard was a mass of rubble and masonry.

He noticed that if you pulled at the wall, more of the brittle material would peel back. After some effort, he had made a hole big enough to crawl into. The boy moved his body sideways to squeeze into the small opening.

He crouched down amongst the rubble and listened carefully to hear if there were any workmen. Then he slowly stood and looked at the house close up. The door with its white pointed archway and windows perfectly painted. The bricks neat and new.

He also remembered that you could reach the back of the house from the right. He turned and peered to see if anyone was there and entered the narrow gap, carefully squeezing through dark shapes of metal, masonry and old bricks.

He crawled out into the sudden grey of the back garden but when he stood, he saw a man wearing a jacket the colour of an orange. The boy crouched back down into a small hole in the dusty debris. The man spat out a jet of phlegm and walked straight past him to the side entrance and edged himself through the gap to the front of the house.

He took one last look at the house and squeezed himself out of the gap and made his way onto Mare Street to head back to Shoreditch.

Among the junk in front of the house, a white rose poked up between two planks of wood, one of its fleshy petals just managing to catch a fleck of sunlight edging over the top of the house. The whole flower stretched out, flexed and opened, the way a woman yawned and woke from a deep sleep.

Find the Page

The morning after he met Erol, Simon looked out at the morning drizzle. Still in his dressing gown and slippers, he hadn't shaved and had no intention to. Staring ahead, he sauntered over to the kitchen and placed his plates into the sink without looking at them, pouring the tap on half-eaten toast.

As he walked over to the bathroom, he felt a tingling in his wrist. He stopped and reached down and massaged it. There was a strange pulsing in his forearm. He thought he could see a lump under the skin. He massaged some more and it disappeared.

Then his right hand twitched. The lumps under his skin started moving around his forearm like baby snakes inside a membrane.

His hand threw his coffee cup against the wall. It jerked upwards and started to tremble. Simon made a fist and it shook from an invisible pressure. It moved to the left and then to the right, flexing away from him as if searching for something in his flat.

His eyes wide now, he tried to resist the hand but it just jerked away, this time to the living room. Simon had no choice but to follow it as his body leapt forward, leaving one of his slippers behind.

The fist darted down; Simon's dressing gown flipped up behind him as he fell to the floor. Against the back wall of the painted-over fireplace, his hand moved to the left and the right as if sniffing like a dog. It stopped in one place.

Then started to scratch. The ends of his fingers scraped at the surface of paint, the sound like nails down a chalk board.

Then they began digging into the wall like some kind of fleshy power tool. Faster and harder. Rodent-like.

Simon could only look in horror as his fingernails began to crack and bleed.

The wall started to smear red, pieces of plasterboard and blood collected in a small pile below what was becoming a large hole in the back of the fireplace.

Soon his fingers met open space. Cold air rushed into the room, along with an unusual smell like matches. Sulphurous. His hand came out and punched a bigger hole.

It jerked in and lower, forcing his body down with it as if he had been pulled by something. His whole forearm was inside the hole and he screamed in agony.

Still inside the hole, his hand stopped with a jerk. When it came out it was clutching something.

Like a swan with a snapped neck, his arm flopped over and his hand opened, dropping the large object to the floor.

Simon fell with his back to the wall. His breathing was now the only sound in the room. He slowed it bit by bit and carefully stood.

He cradled his bloody hand over to the kitchen sink and ran cold water over it. Blood swirled around and into the plug hole. Gradually the pain reduced slightly. Grabbing a paper towel, he wrapped his hand and then walked over to the bathroom, opening the medicine cabinet and pulling down a first aid box. With the injured hand raised, he rummaged around and found a bandage roll with some tape. He carefully wrapped his hand and sat on the toilet seat.

He lifted his phone from his dressing gown and called work. Jill answered.

'Hi, Jill, it's Simon. I'm not feeling too good so I won't be in today. Can you tell David?'

'Sure, Simon. You sound a bit off.'

'Yeah, I couldn't sleep. I think it's this bug that's going round. Tell David if there's anything urgent, I can still work from home. I might need a few days to rest.'

He popped open two codeine pills from the bathroom cabinet, swallowed them and walked over to the fireplace. On the floor, among the debris of white and red dust, was a book. Simon held it up. It was an odd format. Dirty maroon in colour with ripped edges and half the spine missing, it looked extremely old. The cover had gold letters but it was too hard to read. It reminded Simon of those *Boy's Own* books he'd once seen on eBay.

He carefully opened the front cover dangling by a stringy fibre and something flopped out onto the floor.

In the gloom of the living room, Simon peered down to it. It was an old photograph of a group of boys standing in front of a building that seemed familiar. They were dressed in work overalls. Each boy had a strange expression that he couldn't quite pin down; strong but also resigned, melancholy. One of them looked different. He was wearing a cap with his chin cocked forward in defiance. Behind the boys, a huge bald man stood grinning. His hands proudly spread out.

Simon flipped the photo over. Writing was on the back. He held the faded words up to the window then clicked on the kitchen lights.

November 1889

To Arthur Snipe

These words were followed by some strange letters that Simon couldn't distinguish. An *H* then a scribble then a *V* or *Y* with more scribbles.

He looked at the name again. Something about it was unnerving. Familiar.

He got a notification on his phone:

Hi It's Adeolo's mum. I tried to book some lessons but there was something wrong with the app I think. Can you get in touch. Adeolo really liked your lesson.

Simon sat back against the wall with a grunt. He held the phone in his bandaged hand and typed in a new booking and pressed send.

He shuffled over to the bed and heaved the book up with him. He plumped the pillows, placed his head back and breathed out, placing the book to his side, trying to take everything in.

Maybe all this was a social media thing. Some kind of marketing campaign. Was it because I'd entered my email in that publisher's mailing list?

The thought sounded ridiculous the moment it popped into his head. It didn't explain why he had just dug a massive hole in his fireplace, destroying his hand in the process. It didn't explain the fact that he was talking to dead people.

He looked under the bandage, lifting up congealed blood from his forefinger.

'Simon.'

In the shadow of the wardrobe, Erol was sitting on the armchair rolling a spliff.

'Erol, for fuck sake, can you stop doing that.'

'Sorry,' he said with a childish grin across his face as he licked the Rizla paper. 'So, I see you got the book,' he said. His voice low and mellow.

'Well, evidently,' Simon lifted his bandaged hand up.

'Sorry about all the rrrrr.'

He made a gesture with both hands like a rodent.

'Yeah, now my hand's fucked thanks to you.'

'Here, have some of this. It's a good one. It'll help.'

Erol's red Converse high-tops squeaked as he passed the long pointed spliff over.

'I can't believe I'm getting stoned with a fucking ghost now.'

'Now. Take a few drags and it's time for your next job.'

Simon dragged lightly on the joint. He had given up smoking of all kinds years ago and wasn't about to get totally caned while a ghost was in the house. The smell of the smoke took him back. It was hashish. Milder than the psycho-shit kids smoked these days. Hashish?

'How did you get Moroccan hash? A bit retro, Erol.'

'Ah, yes. Membership does have its advantages. Everything I consume is from my era, from the tea to the food, all the way to the gear in my spliffs. It's just the way it works out. Not sure why. Glad you like it, Simon.'

Simon sat back on his pillow and puffed away, the dense smoke filling the room with a blue haze. Horizontal cloudbanks stood still until they were broken apart in slow motion as Simon blew out.

'Simon.'

'Oh, yeah, sorry.'

Simon reached over and handed the spliff back.

'Now. What you have to do next is find Tom. Do you know Giggle?'

'*Giggle*? What's that? A comedy club?'

'You know the map thingy on the you know... the...'

Erol clicked his fingers and pointed in the direction of the dining room table.

'Computer,' Simon finished the sentence.

'Yeah. Computer. Giggle. The search thingy.'

'Oh, you mean Google.'

'Sorry. *Google*. On the...'

'Computer,' Simon said impatiently.

'Sorry, Simon, I'm not very good with these things. Remember, they didn't really exist when I died. They give you a handbook before you come. Sort of training. But it's all a bit baffling to be honest. *Giggle*. Jesus. What a prat. So, yes, go to a *Google* and...' Erol pulled out the palm-sized book from his breast pocket and thumbed through it,

'...ah here. *Find Street View*.'

'Okay, Google Street View, yes,' Simon said.

'What's that?' Erol asked.

'It's a sort of map where you can see the streets as if you're there walking around them.'

'Stone me. Whatever next,' Erol passed the spliff to Simon.

'Well, indeed. I can show you if you like,' he said, taking a drag.

'That's the problem. We're not allowed to. Rules. Something to do with Space and Time and that. It's all above my pay grade that's for sure. I'm just a guide really.'

'Anyway, what's in it for you Erol? Why do you do all this? A sort of penance?'

'Oh, no, it's a points system. The more I help, the closer I get to *Exchange.*'

'Exchange what? Your soul, something like that?'

'God, no. It's an exchange programme. The more tasks I complete here the sooner I can visit. I've got a thing about Victorian London. I've already been once. You haven't lived until you've seen the Thames as Whistler saw it, Simon, honestly. I'm saving up to go again.'

'Sort of like an Erasmus scheme for the undead?'

'Spot on, Simon. If I get Tom back here, I get to go back there.'

'So, this Tom. He's a Victorian ghost?'

'He is. I've got a feeling you'll like him actually.'

'So, what's next?'

'You need to type in this address to the Google thing,' Erol reached over with the little book and showed him a list of numbers, forward slashes and letters and passed him his pencil.

Simon just took a photo of the page with his phone. Erol looked at his pencil and placed it back in his pocket.

'Then what?' Simon said.

Erol thumbed through his booklet again.

'It says, *Find the page.*'

'What's that supposed to mean?' Simon said.

'Search me. It says here... *you'll know it when you see it,*' replied Erol, peering down to the book.

They finished the spliff and Simon eventually drifted off to sleep in a haze of codeine and hash. That afternoon he had the strangest of dreams.

He was in an old cinema of some sort. The type with a band pit down at the front and red curtains pulled back on either side. Every seat was full, the audience concentrating in silence as images of Erol played out on the screen. There was no sound. Some held brass opera glasses. Hash smoke filled the entire theatre.

With a shaky phone camera quality, the white fireplace burst onto the screen to the applause of the audience. The lighting was poor and the images blurry but you could see the scraping and scratching of his hand as the hole became bigger, darker until it filled the screen. The audience began to laugh in silence.

In the seat next to him was a large bald man in a waistcoat. He had an inane grin and was talking continuously into his ear but Simon couldn't hear his words. He was holding one of those old-fashioned walking canes as he spoke.

Simon woke to his cat punching him in the face.

His hand was throbbing and he carefully pulled it out from under his chest with a groan. His mouth was like the inside of an old jar of peanut butter.

He scraped over to the kitchen wearing one slipper, filled the kettle and made a cup of tea. He poured some cat food out for Simon, who duly stuck his head in and crunched away.

Sated, the cat rolled on his back and farted.

'You're welcome,' Simon said.

It was 4:15 and the night was already beginning to claw back the daylight.

Taking a sip of tea, Simon sat down at his dining room table, opened his laptop and breathed out. With his left hand he pulled out his phone and looked down to the numbers. He opened

Google Maps and one-finger typed the address, his bandaged hand resting on the table top.

When the map popped up, his heart stopped. The red arrow marker was on Old Nichol Street right next to his house. He dragged the blue man icon for the Street View page to appear.

He had dropped it at the intersection of Old Nichol Street and Club Row. Familiar streets filled the screen; orange bricked mansion blocks of the Boundary Estate, leaf strewn pavements, the odd cyclist frozen in time, a faceless man with a shopping bag. So far, no page.

Maybe he was supposed to go to a bookshop. There were a few in the area and Simon pulled the view back to try to get his bearings.

He remembered that travelling down Club Row took you back to Arnold Circus and spinning clockwise round the park you could get to Calvert Avenue. He was sure that there was a bookshop up there on the left.

He stumbled along the street looking at each business. The closed shops had shutters buried under layers of graffiti. The open ones, spanking new with brightly lit interiors.

Finally, he found it. *Fandango* — its white-framed entrance and curly red type was what he remembered. He stopped at it and swivelled the camera left then right. Up, down. Zoomed in and zoomed out again. He tried to enter the shop with the Street View camera but it didn't work. Still no page.

He took a sip from his tea and slumped in his chair, moving the mouse aimlessly to the side back up to Arnold Circus.

Then he saw something above the railings of the park that he must have missed first time around. There was a smudge in the air. He zoomed into it.

What looked like a piece of paper was floating just above the wide steps to the raised park.

He zoomed back and around. The object was still there. He moved the camera to the left and closer again and it just hovered in place. He moved the camera up and looked down but as he got closer it simply wobbled and blurred as if the camera movement disturbed its ability to stay in the air; a magnet pulling away from a pole and flexing back in position.

When he moved the arrow away from the park, the object was still at the centre of the camera's view. As he travelled back up Calvert Avenue it travelled with him. However, if he turned a full 180, facing the park again, it disappeared.

When he did this, something in the park caught his eye. A small figure was standing by the bandstand, dressed in a green parka with the hood up. The person was pointing. When Simon followed the finger's direction, it led him back to the floating page at the entrance to Calvert Avenue. He swivelled the camera back to the bandstand but the person was gone. Instead, there was an old woman feeding pigeons with her hands in the air, bread confetti frozen around her. He scrambled the camera away to get a full view of the park again, the mouse scratching away at the table top. The woman was still in the same place but her hands were down and the pigeons were now feeding on the ground. He moved the camera back to Calvert Avenue and the page was there once more.

Simon lurched his mouse along the table like a one-legged sailor looking for the nearest tavern. The page drifted on ahead of him just above the cars in the road. When he reached Shoreditch High Street he stopped and noticed a building just across from the entrance to Calvert Avenue.

He zoomed in and along its length, its black double arches over the first floor with the words *Wells & Company Commercial Iron Works* written across them. A Pret a Manger was at street level. He retrieved the photo from the book and held it up to the screen. It was the same building. The boys looking out of the photo seemed to be staring straight at him now.

Simon swung the camera round and the page was gone again. He panicked and turned around a full 180 degrees in either direction. The person in the parka was now outside Pret a Manger and pointing beyond Shoreditch Church.

The page was floating over the turning to the street and the boy was on the opposite side outside Browns, his hand pointing up Hackney Road. Instead of a blur, like all the other people in the street, the face was shadowed underneath the green hood of the parka and you could just see the white-rimmed sunglasses. Simon followed the page north up Hackney Road to the gasometer by the canal.

Back by Poplar Demand

Simon was woken up by a notification on his phone. When he finally opened his eyes, he realised he had been sleeping for over ten hours. He slid off his bed, smelled his armpits and went to pee.

He clicked a pod into the machine and yawned as he looked at his phone. Adeolo's lesson in Poplar was today at four. He remembered Erol's eyes as they shared the spliff. The map.

As he sipped his coffee he looked at his hand that was beginning to crust over and heal. *If I did everything Erol told me, it would all end. Was that how this was going to work?* Even by Simon's standards that was a little optimistic. Nevertheless, what choice did he have exactly? He knocked back two more codeines and headed to the bathroom.

He carefully peeled away the bandage from his hand and stepped into the shower making sure to not scold it. The hot water instantly made him feel better even though the images of the previous night flashed into his mind as he washed away. He applied a fresh bandage, dressed and headed for the door.

As he stepped onto the street he almost collided with Amanda Saha who was waiting with her arms crossed.

'Hey, what a nice surprise, I was just getting some breakfast would you like to join me?' Simon said.

'We need to talk. You look like shit. What happened to your hand?'

'Oh, just a bit of DIY, you know how clumsy I can get.'

'Really? Simon, you're coming with me.'

'But I've...'

'I'll give you a lift to Poplar. We can talk on the way.'

Amanda opened the passenger door to her Vauxhall and Simon eased himself in as Amanda moved round to the driver's seat.

From a dusty window, Nena looked down at them. She played with the crucifix around her neck as she prayed under her breath. She was still surrounded by unopened boxes.

As they pulled out, Amanda's tone seemed different.

'That search you did. Who was he?'

'Oh, you know just some story I'm following. Why the interest? Once again, really, thanks so much for letting me use...'

'He was murdered. Do you know how?'

'I don't believe I do, Amanda.'

'I think you fucking do, Simon. Has this got anything to do with Kenny's death?'

'Oh, God, no, why would it?'

'Simon, stop bullshitting me. I know you're up to something.'

She looked at his face through the rear-view mirror.

'Simon, you look tired and you're not your little chatty self. Come on, what's going on?'

Simon looked out of the window.

'You wouldn't believe me if I told you. I think I'm going through some sort of... crisis. Anyway, how do you know I'm going to Poplar? That's against the law. Surveillance state and all that. I'm a British tax payer. I pay your bloody wages you know.'

'That's the Simon I know and... Look, don't you worry. We're on the same side here.'

Simon was now looking at her brown eyes in the mirror looking at him. She looked away back to the road.

'Simon. Unfortunately, we have a situation. Your student's mum has got mixed up with someone she shouldn't have. But we can play it to our advantage. Only if you're up for it though.'

She caught his eyes once more in the mirror.

'I don't like getting civilians mixed up in these things. In fact, we are strictly told not to, but I think we've got no choice. It looks like you're already involved whether you like it or not.'

'Ooh I'm feeling better already. Who is it?' Simon just said.

'Hunter Paris. He's getting his hooks right into her and Adeolo. But this is what we're going to do.'

Shove It! Shove It!

That night on the Regent's Canal, a gang of boys cycled past the gasometer, their front wheels parting wisps of fog along the towpath.

One boy threw a bottle into the canal and Jimmy Ballen flipped his front wheel up, balancing back steady and straight as the others laughed. He threw his bike down and unzipped to piss in the canal.

He heard a strange noise from the bushes. He finished his pee, switched on his phone's torch and cast it in the direction of the sound. Through the white haze, the light picked out discarded beer cans and crisp packets stuck in the bushes. The torch caught a movement on the ground.

A stray kitten tangled in a Mulberry bush was mewing for help as it struggled to free itself.

'Here, lads, check this out,' Jimmy said.

They all gathered round.

'What shall we do. Kill it?' one boy said.

'No. I've got a better idea.' Jimmy pulled out a small firework and showed it to the others.

'Yeah. Sick. Blow 'im up,' one boy said rubbing his hands together.

A few yards behind them, a mechanical squeaking echoed from the black tunnel. Light emerged from the darkness, picking out graffiti on the brick arch.

'I know. I'll stick it up its arse,' Jimmy said.

'Yeah', they all screamed.

Jimmy bent down to the cat; the animal was now screaming louder. It hissed and scratched out at the boy as the others laughed.

'Here, you grab 'is head and I'll shove it in.'

Shove it! Shove it! Shove it! they all sang.

As he reached down to the cat, Jimmy noticed something on his hands. At first, he thought it was blood but as he held his hand up to his torch, he realised it was red dust. The type you get from bricks. It tingled on his skin as he tried to rub it off.

Further back down the canal, reflected in the water, a riderless bike's wheels turned faster, the lamps in its spokes flashing. The front wheel went up and the bike wobbled along the path, creating white ribbons of light across black water.

The bike's light poked through the fog shining to where the boys were.

'Someone's comin',' one boy shouted.

The bike spun towards them, slicing the group in half. Three boys fell into the canal. Jimmy was pinned down by the bike. The boys jumped out of the freezing water in a cloud of steam and ran off down the canal screaming.

The bike's tyre was now on Jimmy's throat as it flexed forward. With a strangled scream, the boy reached his arms around the wheel and tried to push the bike off.

A low humming started to come from the spokes as the boy shook, his arms locked on the wheel. The spokes glowed orange and the air became acrid as the tyre began to melt into his face and neck, his arms flailing around.

The bike jerked back and fell over. The glowing spokes hissed and cracked as they cooled in the damp air.

Jimmy's screams echoed under the bridge as he looked at his arms. Singed flesh was melted into his jacket like mozzarella and his hands were blackened and bleeding.

Under the bridge, Tom Baxter in his green parker looked on for a few minutes then turned to head back to Shoreditch.

The Sting

Simon pushed through the entrance of Shoreditch Police Station. It smelt like disinfectant and instant soup. Murmured voices and slamming doors echoed down the hall.

The desk attendant inputted his details into the keyboard and took a headshot with the webcam. The door buzzer sounded and Simon was ushered into a meeting room as he stuck his name tag onto his chest.

Inside, Amanda was sitting at the far end of the desk. Two coffee cups and a note pad sat in front of her. Behind her was a pinboard covered in photographs and a map of the UK. A young policewoman was sitting next to Amanda, pensive and upright. Holding a pen and notepad. Amanda avoided eye contact with Simon.

'Thanks for coming in and helping us with the investigation, Mr Beaver.'

Simon raised his eyebrow to Amanda. She ignored him.

'This is Sergeant Harris. She will be assisting us with the operation.'

'Mr Beaver,' Harris nodded.

'As I said to you before, this is a very unusual situation and you are under no obligation to help us. Are you clear on that, Simon?' Amanda said.

'No. I understand.'

She stood in front of the pinboard.

'Good. This is Hunter Paris. In the past three years he's run around twelve million quid's worth of drugs between these routes in the south west of the country using county lines gangs. Coke, Smack and MDMA mainly. He is responsible for involving over twenty minors in his operation and he has approved at least five murders in the last three years alone. We know he has a safe house in London and we also know it's nowhere near his home address because he's too smart for that.

This is Adaku and her son, Adeolo. We have reason to believe that the boy is being groomed and that the mother is also involved in some way. Coercion, blackmail. In a word cuckooing. We don't know at this early stage. Which brings us to you, Simon.'

Simon sat upright.

'Simon Beaver has been tutoring Adeolo in their home in Poplar and he has potential for getting close to the boy and his mother. Now, we don't need you to do anything, Simon, other than do your job and keep your ears open. Just relay any information about Hunter back to us. That's all. You are not to involve yourself in any way whatsoever that will endanger you. Do you understand, Simon?'

'Think so. What's cuckooing?'

'They're using the home to distribute drugs. The owners are being forced to because they need the money basically. There may be other dynamics to the relationship too, usually are.'

She opened a brown folder on the desk and clicked the pen in her hand.

'I need you to sign this waiver, Simon. It's a confidentiality agreement and it states that you understand the potential danger you will be putting yourself in.'

Simon scanned through the page and signed it, and he slid it back towards her across the desk.

'Great. Do you have any questions?'

'What do you intend doing. What's your goal, if you don't mind me asking?'

'That's a need-to-know thing, but the broad idea is we want to put him away.'

'Simon, when's your next lesson with Adeolo?'

He peered down to his phone and scrolled through his calendar.

'Looks like this week. Wednesday at 4 p.m.'

'As I said, just carry on as normal. No heroics.'

Amanda stood and extended her hand to Simon.

'We'll be in touch and thanks for your help on this.'

Simon stood slowly and the door buzzed. He peeled off the ID and gave it to the duty officer and exited the Police station.

As Simon walked home, the lights of Shoreditch were shining bright once again. Neon bars greeted him with promises of endless fun and adventure that seemed a distant memory right now. A separate world that was out of reach.

He got a text from Amanda.

Sorry about all the amateur dramatics

We can't meet until all this is over

Not safe

Is that OK?

Simon replied.

Sure. I understand

Familiar but Not in a Good Way

Simon woke with a jolt. He looked at his watch. It was around 6 a.m. He flopped around the side of the bed and pulled on his dressing gown. He looked at his face in the bathroom mirror it was grey and drawn. His phone rang.

'Simon speaking.'

'Hi, Simon it's David. Just checking in to see how you're doing. Jill said you were feeling super ill last week. When can we expect you in, the work's stacking up and I need to know if I should get cover. You didn't reply to your emails.'

'I know, David, I'm so sorry. I've not been... feeling so good. But I promise I'll be back next week. Just send anything through you need today. I'm feeling better and I can be more on top of the work now.'

'Only if you're sure, Simon. I'm here to help if you need to talk about anything.'

'Thanks, David, I really appreciate it. I'll be fine, really.'

'Okay, I'll send through a couple of jobs now, if that's Okay?'

'I'll... I'll be ready. Thanks again, David.'

As Simon hung up, he began to cry. He was so embarrassed that he laughed out loud and a line of spittle dripped into his cereal bowl.

He wiped his hand down his greasy face, reached for a paper towel and blew his nose as he stood.

Simon the cat just yawned and rubbed his head against his cat food bag.

That day his focus was laser-sharp. His fingers typing like a machine. By the time he stopped, he had written two articles and sent them back with amendments. He got a mail from David.

He's back!

Thanks, Simon, I'll see you next week.

D

It was already 3 p.m. He hadn't even eaten since the morning and reached over to the fridge and gulped down half a carton of milk.

Out in the busy street, not one sound entered his ears. The people, the traffic, the chaos, all silent like the dream he had had of the theatre.

As he stepped onto the 277, he noticed two things. The smell was familiar but not in a good way and the lower floor was empty except for one passenger. Over at the back, a boy was sitting on his own looking out of the window with a placid expression, as the bus bounced along. The boy was pale with a blue streak of paint down one cheek. He was wearing one of those retro '70s green parkas just like the boy from Street View.

Simon looked behind him as he settled into his seat.

'I suppose you're Tom,' he said.

'That's right. Tom Baxter. Pleased to meet ya, Simon.'

The boy approached him. Simon turned and raised his hands.

'Simon, relax. I'm 'ere to help. With Hunter. The boy. That's why we asked you to take the book to the canal. It's all linked, you'll see.'

'I didn't take the bloody book to the canal, Tom.'

Tom sat next to him. Simon's bones chilled from the inside.

'Ah, but yer did. You just don't remember. It's already 'appened. That's why I'm back. That's why I'm able to speak with yer now. 'Elp you with yer mission.'

'I'm only doing an English lesson, it's not the SAS.'

'What's that?'

'Never mind. Anyway, what are you going to do? Scare him to death.'

'Not exactly. It doesn't work like that with us. It's a little more... creative. It's not an 'Enery James novel if that's what yer mean. Although he did have some good ideas, I'll give 'im that.'

He resumed his gaze out of the window.

'So, what do I do?'

'Nothin'. Just do your lesson and we'll take care of the rest. You really remind me of someone I used to know, Simon.'

'Oh, yeah. Who's that, Tom?'

'Do you like electricity, Simon? I do. I do *love it so*. It really is magic, isn't it. All of this,' he gestured to the traffic lights and cars reflected in the shop windows.

As the bus slowed in the traffic, Tom watched a homeless man smoothing his black greasy hair down with an old comb. He was using the window of a restaurant as a mirror as he grinned away.

'It's strange to me, Simon. London has changed so much while staying exactly the same. All the advances, all the inventions. All that knowledge. Why is that, Simon?'

'Not really given it much thought, Tom. Oh, by the way I wanted to show you this.'

Simon pulled out the photo of the boys in front of the factory. As he showed Tom, a look of sadness crossed his young face.

'Who are they?'

'We worked in a paint factory right here. These are my friends.'

He touched the photo as he spoke.

'Who's the big fella? He looks familiar.'

'That's Arthur Snipe. Our boss. He was a bad person, Simon. Really bad.'

Tom turned the photo over in his hand. The lights on the bus flickered and dimmed. His eyes swivelled up and turned as black as coal. A hissing, like dry sand pouring out of a bag came from Tom's open mouth as red dust filled the space in front of his face. All you could see were his black eyes poking through the red mist. All Simon could do was move further against the window as the burnt smell became stronger.

On the back of the photo the words started to move around as the hissing got louder. The letters dissolved and re-arranged, moving up and down and across like a crossword.

It now read:

November 2022

To Hunter Paris

Henry VIII

The photo caught fire and fell. Simon stamped on it, the ashes mixing with the wet dirt on the floor of the bus.

The lights went up again and the bus stopped, letting more passengers on. As they sat down, they covered their faces from the toxic burning stench.

Doolally

Simon walked across the hamster tube to Poplar trying to focus on the lesson ahead. *Just a normal lesson. Everyday work. Normal. Normal. Normal.*

On the other side, he looked back to the hamster tube and down to the stairs hoping to see Erol before taking the first steps down to the estate. The yellow street lights gave the road a sickly submerged feel that he hadn't notice before.

He was walking fast and the minute he became conscious of this fact slowed down. Despite the chilly air, clammy sweat lingered on the back of his neck. He climbed the steps of the estate and walked along the exterior hall and knocked.

He could hear a male voice from behind the door and tensed his head up and waited. His mouth curdling to cotton wool.

Adaku came to the door wearing her pinny, hands in the air, white surgical gloves covered in meat.

'Come in. Sorry, I was just making some food for later.'

Simon moved through the hallway looking to his right and left.

'You alright, Simon?'

'Oh, yes, couldn't be better.'

'How's your hand? On the mend I hope.'

'Yeah, much better now.' He craned his neck into the living room. The TV was on and a male presenter was loudly interviewing a politician.

'Sorry about the TV, I leave it on when I'm pottering around the flat.' She grabbed the remote and switched it off.

Adeolo was drawing pictures on a big white pad. Coloured pencils and papers were spread all over his desk.

'Hi, Simon.'

'Hey, mate,' Simon said.

'Put your stuff away and get your books out, Adeolo,' Adaku said as she walked back to the kitchen.

Adeolo handed one of his pictures up to Simon.

'This is for you.'

It was a picture of man with a bandaged hand and a little belly. In his other hand was a book.

'Adeolo, I love it. Who is it?' He winked as he carefully placed the drawing into his notebook.

'Very funny. So, what are we gonna do today, Simon?'

'Well, I thought we could do some creative writing. How does that sound?'

'Cool.'

As Adeolo scooped up his drawings, one of them fell to the floor and Simon bent to pick it up. It was of a man wearing a cap, driving a car. Adeolo had drawn the Mercedes symbol at the front.

'Who's this one of, Adeolo?'

'It's Hunter. He's our friend. He helps Mum. Bought this TV for us.'

Adaku entered the room.

'What did I tell you, Adeolo? Don't talk about other people unless they know them. It's bad manners. Tea, Simon?'

'Yes, please.'

Simon shared some printouts with Adeolo and they began their lesson.

As Adeolo scribbled in his notepad, Simon looked around the room to see if anything was out of place. Apart from the curtain looking new, everything seemed normal. He looked out of the door to the hall.

Adaku called in from the kitchen. 'Adeolo, I've got to get something from the shops. I'll be back in 10 minutes.'

'Alright, Mum,' he shouted back.

The front door slammed.

Simon looked out of the room again.

'I've got to use the bathroom, mate.'

'Sure,' Adeolo said without looking up from his work.

Simon walked towards the toilet cubicle and looked back before passing it and walked down the hall. There was a bedroom to the right with the door half open, opposite was a room with posters on the wall that he took for Adeolo's. At the end of the hall was another closed door.

He reached for the handle and turned it, but it was locked. He pushed, but it stayed in place.

When he turned, Adeolo was standing behind him.

'What you doing, Simon? The loo's this way. You know, you've been here loads of times.'

'I know, mate, I'm on these pills for my hand they're making me go a bit doolally.'

'*Doolally*, what's that?'

As they walked back to the toilet, he jumped into the air.

'Well, it's a bit like when you lose your mind because your student keeps following you around and then you go a bit craaaaaazy.' Simon put on his best crazy face which made Adeolo laugh.

'I'll be just a sec, mate. Get back to your story. What was I thinking? Honestly.'

'You weren't thinking, Simon.'

'You know what? You're not wrong.' He slipped into the cubicle and pretended to pee.

Eventually, Adaku returned. She was talking as she entered. Simon heard a man's voice.

'Hunter's here!' Adeolo said smiling.

'You should meet him, Simon, he's got a sick motor.'

'Hello, big man,' Hunter said to Adeolo ignoring Simon.

'Hunter, I've done a drawing of you. Look.'

He handed the picture over.

'That's well cool, mate. Very talented. I like the car too. Can I keep it?'

'Yeah, it's for you.'

Hunter took the picture and put it to one side.

'Alright,' he said to Simon half ignoring him as he returned to the kitchen.

As the lesson continued, Simon tried to listen to their conversation as they cooked. They seemed to be getting along well, laughing and joking with each other.

Hunter returned with plates and cutlery and placed them down on the table. Simon got ready to leave. Hunter turned to him.

'Here, don't I know you from somewhere?'

'I work... for a newspaper in Hackney. The Resident. My photo's been in it a couple of times, maybe it's that. We gave an award. For a statue.'

Simon thought he answered too quickly.

'Nah. Not that. It's something else,' Hunter said rubbing his jaw.

'Maybe I've got one of those faces,' Simon said smiling.

'What faces?'

'Familiar,' Simon swallowed. Hunter was now staring directly at him. His face was close to his. Simon pretended not to notice and pulled his bag up from the floor and turned to leave.

'You did well today, Adeolo. See you next week.'

'See you, Simon,' Adeolo said with a wave.

'Simon who?' Hunter asked.

'Simon Beaver.'

'See you around, *Simon Beaver*.'

Simon could feel Hunter's eyes following him as he left.

As he ate, Hunter kept looking around the room, ignoring Adeolo and his mum. Distracted, he finished his food quickly then pretended to look at a message on his phone and stood to leave.

'Listen. I've got to run. Something's come up at the shop. The food was great. It's my treat next time. Alright, Adeolo?'

He fist bumped him.

As Hunter rushed to the door, Adeolo called over to him.

'Hey, Hunter, you forgot your drawing!'

'So I did, mate, sorry.'

He scooped it up and folded it away in his jacket.

'Thanks, Picasso,' Hunter called over as he slammed the door. Down in the estate's car park, he looked up to the flat as he started the engine and called Max.

'We might have an issue. Meet me at Ling's now.'

As Hunter pulled out of the estate, he crumpled Adeolo's drawing into a ball and threw it out of the window. It sank into a puddle as he drove off down to Bow.

Ling's

Ling's was packed. Hunter had to look around the whole restaurant to find Max. He finally spotted him sitting at the back jamming food into his big gob. A full table of noodles and rice sat in front of him. Hunter squeezed between the crowded tables and edged in beside him.

'What's up, Hunter?'

'Do you ever stop eating, you fat cunt?'

'It's free, Hunter.'

'Listen.'

He looked around and lowered his voice. Max put his fork down.

'There's a nosy cunt round the Poplar place.'

'Do you want me to sort it, bruv?'

'Not yet. I want you to look into a Simon Beaver. He's a journalist for the Hackney Resident. Find out where he lives. Everything. You get me.'

'Done, Hunter.'

'We need to be more careful now. Any news on Kenny?'

'Na, bruv. It's like he disappeared or somethin'. Maybe he got done by that E8 lot and they buried 'im.'

'No. Not their style. Keep lookin' and get that info about Simon Beaver ASAP. How are the other lot?'

'They've all left for Bristol, two others are already in Cornwall. The safe house is set up. That Jill is well nice there.'

'Max, make sure you don't get involved. Don't be a prat. It's just business. Use your head and not that one.'

He pointed down to his crotch.

'Course, bruv.'

With that, Hunter was gone just as soon as he'd arrived.

Back at his flat, Simon twisted open a beer. He sent a text to Amanda. His thumbs moving fast over the keypad.

I think he suspects something

He was acting weird

Confrontational

He asked my full name

Where I work

Amanda replied.

Just act like u know nothing

Getting more intel 4u

Keep u posted

A

He felt comforted but not sure why. He wanted to continue the chat but had nothing more to say and placed his phone face down on the table.

The cat jumped down and hid under the bed.

Then Simon smelt the burning. He knew what was about to happen. By now he was quite relaxed about the whole ghost thing. It was amazing how you could get used to something so strange so quickly.

'Evenin', Simon.'

Tom Baxter was standing with his back to him by the window. His parka hood hanging down behind his head.

'Tom. You made it. What took you so long?' Simon asked.

'Oh, ya know. Things to do. People to see. I'm a busy man these days.'

He peeked out through the curtains as he spoke.

'Can't believe what they did to the old neighbourhood. Don't recognise it. Looks nice though. Real tidy like. The trees. Park.'

'So, Erol, he's gone to...' Simon asked.

'Yeh, London. 1888. We exchanged. He's a good sort, Erol. I hope he didn't scare ya. We didn't mean ta.'

'Oh, no. Well, at first, I was shitting it. But after a while you just...'

'Adjust. Yes. I know exactly what ya mean, Simon.'

'I think Hunter knows I'm up to something, Tom.'

'Good. Keep 'im thinkin'. Distracted. That's what we like.'

'If you say so. What now, Tom?'

'Well, we wait. Just go ta your next lesson. That's when things will start ta get interestin'. But for now, I'd like a tour if you don't mind. Only if you've the time, Simon.'

'A tour? What of?'

'The lights.'

Tom turned and his black eyes blinked in the gloom. The reflections of Simon's lamp looked like white pin pricks in two black universes.

Welcome to Barbados

As Simon led him to Bethnal Green Station, Tom looked in all directions. He pulled his hood up. Put on his sunglasses.

'Simon, what are these everywhere? Are they signs?'

'Oh, that. It's just graffiti. A mixture of gang tags, art, culture. All sorts of stuff mixed up. Why? Do you like it?'

'Yes, it's strange. Very colourful. So, the gangs are Italian? From the Latin *graffito*, I think it means scratch or somethin'.'

'No, they're *all* nationalities, Tom. That's something you might have to get used to. London. *The world.* It's become international. It's called globalisation. Everyone is everywhere. All the time. In fact, some people say Britain invented it.'

'How interestin',' Tom said as he stopped and stared at a multi-coloured duck holding a machine gun. He gazed up to the railway bridge at the electric wires strung above the track. As the trains came and went, blue sparks played across them with a lovely fizz.

They went down into the station and the hot wind blew up the stairs. Tom looked at the blue card that Simon bought him not really knowing why it was called O-Y-S-T-E-R. He Turned it around in his hand and they approached the strange gates.

Simon tapped a metal box next to the gate, passed through it and waited for Tom on the other side.

'You tap it here and the things open for you automatically.'

Tom tapped his card and walked through the open jaws of the barrier, he looked behind him as he passed through. He jumped back as they clunked closed once again.

Then Simon showed him another staircase that went down. It was a most strange moving thing. Tom stepped on and then stepped off it right away, shaking his head. Simon ran back up as the machine tried to take him down, and helped Tom onto the first step. As they went down Tom preferred to sit. Simon quickly pulled him up as they approached the bottom. Tom stared back at the steps disappearing into the ground.

On the platform Tom looked up at the curved roof lights along the length of the tunnel and he held his ears as the train screeched in.

He watched Simon's finger as he pressed the lamp on the door and it slipped open. Tom looked left and right then inside before stepping up to the carriage.

They managed to get a seat on the crowded train and Tom lurched back in his seat as it screamed forward and the dark tunnel shot past through the windows. He looked up at Simon and round at everyone. They seemed not to care and instead either looked at their rectangular looking glasses or simply stared into the air.

A woman looked up from her glass and smiled at Simon as she watched them both.

'First time on the tube?' She said.

'Yeah. It's all new for him he's not from... this... here,' Simon replied.

To take his mind off the noise, Tom looked up to the strange notices along the inside of the train. So many messages. Wares. Things to buy. How can anyone decide when faced with so much choice?

'Simon?' Tom asked quietly.

'Yes, Tom.'

'What's Coca-Cola?' he whispered out of the side of his mouth.

'It's a drink. Very refreshing. Sugary. You drink it when you're thirsty. I'll buy you one when we get there.'

'Where are we going anyway?'

'It's a surprise, Tom. You're going to love it.'

They jumped off the red line at the station at Holborn and headed through a tunnel. People rushing this way and that flew past them. The bodies had their own rhythm. Speed. If you went as fast as them you wouldn't crash into anyone but if you slowed down, you would come a cropper that's for sure. Maybe that's what Simon meant by globalisation. Everyone moving in one direction like a big people machine. Forward motion at all times whether you liked it or not.

They got on the blue line. On it there were people with travel luggage, oriental fellows and families. The train only stopped a few times and Simon gestured for him to get off.

They turned to a tunnel and joined another moving staircase. Simon steadied Tom as they jerked up and people on the other side jerked down. Tom tried not to laugh as the feeling of movement vibrated through him as dashes of light played over his sunglasses.

When they stepped off the moving stairs Tom looked across a wide room with lots of other gates. They walked through one and Simon led him to another small staircase.

The air rushed down like cold vinegar as they climbed the steps. When they reached the top, Tom grabbed Simon's hand. Initially he pulled it away but then gripped it.

The first surprise was the brightness. The underground train station had been dark and Shoreditch itself had been rather dark too. This, on the other hand, was something quite different.

High up, he saw a giant glowing picture that moved as if people — giant people — were inside it. They were on a tropical beach of some sort and frolicked in the water, bathed in bright sunshine. Words that moved around the picture said 'Welcome to Barbados. Welcome to Paradise'.

'Are we in Barbados, Simon?'

'No. That's an advert to go to Barbados on holiday. We're in Piccadilly Circus.'

'Oh, I've been to the Dilly. I see it now. What's that?'

'It's the statue of Eros.'

'B-O-O-T-S,' Tom mouthed the words, looking across the way.

'So there's a shoe shop. I think that was there before. Looks much bigger than how I remembered,' he said.

As he held Simon's hand they walked to another big road coming off the circus. The line of lamps above it looked like lightning frozen along its whole length. There were hundreds of people walking around, more than he had ever seen in his life. Some stopped and held up their rectangular looking glasses and eyed them as they circled them round the lights. Some held sticks that raised the glasses even higher.

'Simon, why does everyone carry a looking glass with them?' he said pointing.

'Oh, those. They're telephones. They allow you to speak to another person in a different place. You can hear their voice and they can hear yours. Even a different country. They're very useful.'

'What's wrong with writing a letter? I don't understand. Have you got one, Simon?'

'Yeah, look.' He pulled his out and showed him.

'You can even take a photograph with it,' Simon said.

'What's a photy-graph? You mean like a camera obscura? Thought you said it was a telly-phone, Simon?'

'It's both. Look.'

Simon lifted it up and showed Tom the image of the street sign of Regent Street and pressed the button then lifted it back for Tom to see.

Behind his sunglasses, Tom's black eyes stared down and touched the shiny surface. His hand flexed up as the photy-graph became bigger on the small glass.

As they curved along Regent Street, Tom noticed a big shop window full of books. He pulled Simon's hand to stop there.

'Can we go in?' he pleaded.

'Course, Tom.'

Tom looked around the large room. In some ways it reminded him of Mr Tipps's shop, but in others it was so different. He had never seen so many books in one place in his entire life.

On a central display was a big notice with many copies of one particular book. The cover was the colour of a dark orange. The black title like curly leaves. He had seen it before somewhere. Maybe from Tipps, he couldn't remember.

Simon noticed Tom staring at the display.

'Songs of Innocence and *Songs of Experience* by William Blake. I used to read this as a kid.'

'What's a kid, Simon?'

'Sorry, I mean as a child. My mother used to read it to me.'

'What's it about?'

'Well, it's kind of about the natural state of human beings. William Blake writes that we are born innocent until experiences change us, usually for the worse, I'm afraid.'

Tom edged towards the display and picked one up and opened it. His black eyes widening behind his sunglasses as he read. His lips moving as his finger followed each word. The page showed an illustration of a fierce tiger hiding in a forest.

'It's funny, I used to read the stories in a different order depending on what mood I was in,' Simon added.

Tom was in silence as he stared at the page.

'Do you want it, Tom? I can buy it if you like.'

'Really? Isn't it expensive?'

'Let's see.'

He picked up a copy and flipped the little hardback book over. It was on sale. Fifty per cent off.

'It's only five pounds, Tom. I'll get it for you if you really like it.'

'Five pounds? Are you rich, Simon?'

'Course not,' Simon said laughing as he picked up a copy and headed to the till.

Through the shop window a man watched them, his face in shadow under his hoodie. He took a photograph and walked away from the brightness of the window.

He sent a text with the picture.

He's got a kid wot shall I do?

Max

The reply came back.

Keep on him back 2 boundary

Text me when u get there

H

'Where next, Simon?' Tom asked.

'Well, I thought we, I mean I, should be getting back. I've got work to catch up on and I'm seeing Adeolo again tomorrow. He's got a test coming up.'

'Oh, yes, I understand,' Tom answered as he looked to the pavement and then back up to the advertising screen once more.

'We can go again, Tom. Or go to other places if you like. There's so much to see and everything's changed so much that you wouldn't believe it.'

But when Simon turned around Tom was nowhere to be seen. He realised he was still holding the little book.

'You forgot your book, Tom. Tom?'

That night Simon sat in his flat with just a reading lamp for company. As he read, the sound of the words were in his mother's voice.

The Last Lesson

At Poplar, Adeolo was on good form. He insisted on drawing every word that was included in his test preparation instead of concentrating on the test itself.

'Why do I get the feeling you're not taking this seriously, Adeolo?'

'Can't think why that is, Simon. I am one of your most *dedicated* students,' he said, highlighting the vocabulary he had to use while also drawing an elephant playing a PS5.

'Okay, I see what you're doing. Now you're making fun of me.'

'Me? Never. I would never do that. Don't *underestimate* me,' he said, pointing to the word *underestimate* in his book.

'Very funny. I need a break, Adeolo. Make me a tea, mate. Pleeeease?'

'Okay, boss, anything to stop doing this silly lesson,' he said jumping down off his chair and heading to the kitchen.

As he made the tea Simon lurked around the kitchen doorway and looked to the right. The door which had been locked was now half open and he could make out the white boxes piled up inside.

Simon heard a clicking in the lock as Adeolo's mum came through the door.

Instead, Max entered. He was carrying a sports bag.

'Hey, big man.'

Adeolo dropped the tea bag on the kitchen top and ran to him.

'It's Max, Hunter's friend!'

'Alright,' Max said looking to the floor, ignoring Simon as he pulled his hood back and loped down the hall to the room.

'So, where's my tea?' Simon asked as he settled back into his chair in the living room looking back to the hall.

Adeolo shuffled through carrying the big mug with both hands.

From the hall Simon could hear the sound of scraping and rattling. Boxes being shoved about.

Adeolo noticed Simon listening.

'Aren't we going to continue with the lesson, Simon?'

'Course we are, mate. It's just that you're so good now, you know everything.'

He looked at his watch and sipped his tea.

'Tell you what. If you can spell the next three words, we can call it a day.'

'Okay, Simon, you're on.'

'When is your mum coming back?' he said as he looked to the door.

'Dunno, she's late. Went shopping.'

He looked at his watch once more.

'Okay, so we've got five minutes. I just need you to do one thing.'

'What's that, Simon?'

'Do you like games? We're going to play one.'

He put his finger to his mouth.

'I want you to hide until your mum comes back. We're going to both hide, in fact,' he whispered.

'Okay? This is a weird spelling test, Simon.'

'Come, it'll be fun. Down here, look.'

He pulled out the TV on its trolley and gestured behind it.

'Now, this is the first word. *Instantly.*'

'That one's easy. I-N-S-T-A-N-T-L-Y.'

'Okay. Now, *instantaneous.*'

'Okay. The adjective. That one's a bit harder.'

Just then Max entered the room.

'What the fuck are you two doing down there?'

'It's a spelling test. I know. Simon's a bit weird, Max,' Adeolo said tapping his head.

'Listen. Adeolo, I need to tell you something. Come 'ere,' Max replied.

Simon looked at his watch once more.

There was a crash at the door.

Adeolo's face jumped, his eyes wide.

Max turned.

In a split second the flat was full of police.

Max just stared at Simon who was now shielding Adeolo behind the TV.

Two shots were fired.

The Party at Snipe's, 1889

One side of St Paul's dome was lit up, the other blackened in shadow. The Bank of England's columns appeared and disappeared like prison bars in a giant's jail. At the base of the building, the rain-spattered dragon tongues on the City of London's crest licked like flames.

Over at the warehouse in Shoreditch, Bert's piano notes, like a tin can rolling down cobble stones, repeated the last chorus of an old favourite.

A door on bricks was the bar, on top of which pickled onions and whelks sat. Arthur Snipe leaned toward Theodore Hush, telling another anecdote, tankard in hand.

As the next song started, Snipe couldn't help himself and leaped up, singing along, spittle flying out of his mouth, pointing his thumbs to his chest, dancing with his knees up in the air.

I'm 'Enery the Eighth, I am,
'Enery the Eighth I am, I am!
I got married to the widow next door,
She's been married seven times before.

He dragged Hush to the piano, Hush stiffly singing along, as the other workers grabbed his shoulders in a sweaty embrace that was more fight than dance. Alice linked arms with Hush as she sang.

And every one was an 'Enery
She wouldn't have a Willie nor a Sam
I'm her eighth old man named 'Enery
'Enery the Eighth, I am!

Tom and the boys had been drinking beer like the adults and Curly had already vomited into one of the guest's hats that he'd found behind the piano. Sticks was now chasing the other four boys around with it, they threaded between the other guests shouting at the top of their voices.

More people arrived, their dark coats and hats covered in silvery dots of rain. Each time the warehouse door opened, a gust of wind blew in to the hot space, making the score sheet on Bert's piano flutter as he steadied it with one hand and deftly played away with the other. Every time he counted-in a new verse, he threw his head back, baring a mouth of destroyed teeth.

The Chinese from Limehouse huddled together humming along and tapping their feet. One of them had a monkey on his shoulder and the creature chattered and clicked away as it reached for the pies on top of the piano, flakes of pastry dropping down on to Bert's bowler hat.

As the song ended, a breathless Alice, her sweating bosoms heaving, made an announcement.

'That song was dedicated to a Mr Arthur Snipe, the king of the Old Nichol! It's time for a short interlude before the next song. It looks like a storm's coming so stay here, have a drink, have a pie and whatever you do, have a bloody good time! We shall return in just a tick.'

Bert carefully lowered the lid on his piano and they both headed to the bar as the guests raised their glasses.

The warehouse was beginning to fill up with the great and the good of East London. Boxers rubbed shoulders with petty thieves, musicians talked excitedly with working ladies and barmaids. There was a bald man with a big moustache, holding a giant snake around his shoulders and Tom and the lads carefully touched it as it slithered across his chest. The sound of everyone's voices echoed up and around the high ceiling so it was almost impossible to hear what anyone was saying.

Unnoticed by all, the blue doors of the 'frey's laboratory were ajar.

A refreshed Bert and Alice returned to the piano to the applause of everyone gathered. Bert sat at his piano and shuffled through his score sheets as they discussed the next song. Some sheets fell to the floor and he bent over to gather them up, shuffling them into place before they started.

'Hurry up, we haven't got all night!' a man at the front shouted.

Quick as whip, Alice responded.

'Is that what your boyfriend said last night?'

The whole room erupted with laughter. Even the heckler couldn't help himself.

'Now, everyone knows this one.'

Bert counted in.

Lately I just spent a week with my old Aunt Brown,
Came up to see wond'rous sights of famous London Town.
Just a week I had of it, all round the place we'd roam
Wasn't I sorry on the day I had to go back home?
Worried about with packing, I arrived late at the station,
Dropped my hatbox in the mud, the things all fell about,
Got my ticket, said 'good-bye.' 'Right away,' the guard did cry,
But I found the train was wrong and shouted out…

By now everyone was singing along as the chorus exploded.

Oh! Mister Porter, what shall I do?
I want to go to Birmingham
And they're taking me on to Crewe,
Send me back to London as quickly as you can,
Oh! Mister Porter, what a silly girl I am!

Tom and the lads were joining in. They danced around, elbows raised as the crowd sang as one. The boys linked arms, their faces sweating as they jumped this way and that. Tom forgot about all his worries. His mum and dad. The book. He even forgot about Vanessa. It was as if every moment had slowed down and each second was a moment of pure joy.

The song ended. Breathless, the boys headed to the bar. As they were waiting for their drinks, the atmosphere seemed to change. The crowd in the middle of the room gave way to a group of ladies with dark dresses, made-up hair, leather boots, frilly petticoats and wild hats. All had fancy make-up with dark eyes, faces of white powder, lips of crimson red. It was the Hoxton lot. They clustered together as one, some fanning themselves as the room got a little hotter.

Lefty jabbed Tom in the stomach.

'Look at that. Lovely. Which one are you 'avin', Tom?'

'Do I have to choose?' Tom said, in a mocking, dreamy sort of way.

'Here, that one's lookin' at ya, Tom. Think she likes you.'

Tom looked sideways as subtly as he could.

'Mum. What you doing here?'

The question was heard by everyone close to them and two burly men, leaning at the bar, mimicked Tom's words.

'That's a good one, Tom,' Sticks said, laughing.

'Yeah, Mum what you doin' here?' Curly repeated the joke.

Another group started to laugh near them.

'No really, what you doin' here, Mum?'

Tom looked up at Anne Baxter as she broke away from the other women and ran to the back of the warehouse.

Tom turned to Righty in panic, Lefty reached out to Tom to console him but Tom had already bolted after her. The rest of the boys realised what had just happened and huddled together, each boy looking to the door and turning inwards to talk under their breath. Some of the guests were either laughing, whispering or repeating Tom's words.

Tom cornered her in a dark hall at the back of the warehouse. She was looking down to her feet.

'I didn't know where they was taking me until it was too late. I'm sorry, Tom. I didn't know. He said we was going to a pub and then they changed their mind and came here. What was I supposed to do?'

'Mum, what do you mean? Who told you? I thought you was with the nuns in Mare Street.'

'It's complicated, Tom. I met some other women there and they said they'd help me. They introduced me to... some people.'

'What people, Mum?'

Anne looked to the floor, fiddling with a button on her blouse. She then looked up, her face changed, looking past Tom.

There were three metallic taps on the wall, like someone knocking on a door.

'I suppose you two know each other?' a voice boomed over in the corner.

A smiling Arthur Snipe leaned casually against the wall, one hand on his hip as if he was a man bringing flowers to a Christening.

Tom said nothing. He then ran at Snipe, arms punching wildly. One of his fists caught his chin with a slap, and it seemed to just bounce off without any impact. Snipe reached down and held Tom's head in place as the boy's arms flailed around like a drowning man.

'Easy, Tom, you'll do yourself a mischief, mate. I was only trying to help.'

'You only want ter help yourself. You know it,' Tom screamed.

'Tom, careful,' Anne shouted.

'Look, Tom, all the money she makes is far more than your five shillings, so what is all the fuss about? I really don't understand.'

'You *know* why. You're sick, Mr Snipe. You're not right in the 'ed everyone knows that. You just take and take until there's nothin' left for anyone else. I'm sick of it. Sick of it, see?'

Tom had slipped to the ground with his back to the wall, cradling his legs, his knees against his face, as he rocked backwards and forwards sobbing.

Snipe reached down and touched Tom on his head.

'Get away from me, you cunt. You fucking cunt, Snipe. I'll kill you. I'll fucking stab you in yer eye.'

'I'm sorry, Mr Snipe, he doesn't mean it. Did you, Tom? He's just a bit emotional about his dad, aren't you?' Anne said.

Snipe nodded to Anne and went back to the party; she bent down and stroked his hair.

'Tom, it's not going to be forever. I promise. Just every now and again.'

Tom stopped sobbing as his breathing became more even and calm.

But then he looked up to his mother as if she was made of glass. He removed her hands from his and placed his own by his side, stood for a moment staring into space.

'Tom, I'm at that house if you want to chat. I'm always there for you. You know that, don't you? Whatever happens.'

Tom just looked into the space in front of him.

'It looks like a storm's coming, I best be leaving,' she said after a long silence.

Anne Baxter left by the back entrance, looking up to the sodden sky and used the rainwater to wipe the make-up from her face. The water poured down her cheeks as she hurried back to Mare Street.

Tom just continued staring ahead as he returned to the party. Around him, everyone danced, laughed and drank away, but to him all was silence. The only noise in his ears was a low thrumming tone, growing from within. He walked through the crowd, like a floating head without a body. He noticed that he was shaking lightly and all his thoughts were mixed in his head. There seemed to be no way to see clearly to the future. His thoughts were trapped and his head had become a jail where all the events of his life fought like mad prisoners. Where no one could escape. No one could survive.

He was brought back into the room by Sticks's voice.

'Don't worry, Tom, he's a wanker. He'll get his, don't you worry,' he said as he carefully smiled over at Snipe who was laughing and joking with someone by the piano.

Curly put his arm round Tom's shoulder and passed him a bottle of beer.

''Ere. Get this down you.'

Tom took the bottle and drank a large gulp.

'I got a knock on 'im you know?' Tom said.

'Snipe? You jokin'?'

'Yeah, he was shocked. Couldn't believe it.'

'Good for you, Tom,' Lefty said looking over his shoulder.

Tom lifted his bottle.

'To the boys.'

'The boys!'

They all drank back slugs of beer. Lefty let out a massive belch.

'It's not your fault, Tom. For all I know, my mum's on the game too,' Curly said.

There was a short silence before all four boys burst into laughter. Righty squirted beer out of his nose he was laughing so hard. Even Tom let himself have a little smile.

Curly gestured to the pantry.

'Lads. I've got an idea. Come over 'ere.'

They all followed him, looking at each other with interest.

As they entered the narrow room, Curly poked his head out of one end to see if anyone was looking, closed the door, stood on a beer keg and reached for something in the cupboard. It was a tall narrow tin with bright green letters over the front.

''Ere, Tom, what's this say?'

BANISH

CONSTIPATION

- WITH -

BROOKLAX

THE BRITISH BROOKLAX
CHOCOLATE LAXATIVE
GET THINGS MOVING AGAIN

'It's for when you can't crap,' Tom replied.

'Thought so. Jon puts it in his tea every morning. Why don't we put it in Snipe's beer tonight?' Curly said.

'Yeah!' they all said as one.

Tom stood in front of the boys and began to talk.

'In fact, I've been thinking, boys. Snipe needs to learn a lesson and not just this way. We need to use the lightning. Tonight's the night.'

'What you mean, Tom?' Sticks asked.

'See that storm beginning outside? That's our chance. I've put everything in place and it might as well be tonight. It's all nice and ready for him.'

The boys looked at each other with excited but confused faces.

Simon

Hunter Paris checked his Apple watch. Took a sip of water and stretched against the wall as he looked out to the white dots across the river.

Fucking Max. Should've gone himself then none of this would've happened. Still, he was free and Max was in the nick. Deal with it later. Pity about the boy tho. He had potential that one. There'll be others.

At least the feds fucked up. Nothing there for them to see. But the house is fucked too. Knew there was something about that teacher. Always right. The fucker saw too much tho. Got to sort it.

Jay's on it. Should be an easy hit. Homerton's not far. All nice and tidy. Teachers, who needs those cunts anyway?

He put his earbuds in and pressed play — Loski, 'On Me'. Moved over to the treadmill and stretched his calf then each arm behind his back.

Then he saw a flicker by the treadmill in the reflection in the window. It looked like a blue light. *Couldn't be all the way up here tho.* He moved to the window and squinted as far down into the street as he could by pressing his face against the window. Nothing. Then jumped up to the machine and tapped in his workout settings.

He felt good the moment the machine started up. Blood moving around. Breathing evenly. The music's rhythm began to sync with his pumping legs. He increased the speed as his heart rate increased with it. He looked at himself in the dark window as he ran. Moved his face from one side to another, raising his jaw. He placed his phone in the treadmill cubby hole and increased the speed.

The rectangles of light at the entrance of Homerton Hospital blurred into the icy air. A woman helped a patient on crutches out of the double doors of A&E and across the car park, steam rising from their mouths as they reached for their car keys.

The automatic doors slid open. Simon Beaver walked across to the bus stop. It wasn't long before the bus came. He sat with a pained grunt, popped two pain killers and glugged a sip of water from a small bottle as the driver jerked away.

It was now pitch-black outside. The smeared windows making everything outside seem slow and distant. It reminded Simon of how it felt to drive at night wearing sunglasses. Shapes came and went, cyclists floated past and traffic lights flared through drizzly dots.

After a few stops the pills began to work and he settled back into his seat and adjusted his sling. He could only just feel the pain on the side of his arm.

Simon Beaver. Intrepid tutor. Shot in the line of duty. Amanda had said it just grazed him. Low calibre. It would make a great story. I might pitch it to David next week. Talk about a journalist making a story.

A feeling of deep sadness rose up as the pain killers pushed down.

Adeolo. Wrong place at the wrong time. Poor lad.

He felt a presence from a seat to his left. Eyes watching.

He casually glanced over. A man in an Adidas hoodie was face down, engrossed in a video on his phone. Simon thought he saw him glance up briefly.

The only other passenger was a woman sitting directly behind him, wearing an abaya with her phone tucked in her headscarf as she talked away quietly looking out of the window.

Hunter heard his doorbell ring through the music. At first, he thought it was part of the track. He took out his earbuds, paused the song and pressed the stop button on the treadmill. Slowly the rhythmic bang of the road came to a halt and the lights on the display went out. Before opening the door, he stretched up above the Henry VIII painting and pulled down a small pistol.

He reached for the door and held the weapon down by his side.

He rocked back and forth before opening up. Blood pumping adrenalin. He opened the door fast but no one was there. Looked down the hall and to the left. He heard another door open and close in the communal hall. He tapped his door shut and double locked it.

When he returned to the treadmill it was running again, shaking as the endless road spun round with rhythmic thumps. The lights on the control pad flashing. He looked behind himself slowly, calmly reached up to turn it off and its thumps slowed down to a stop.

The flat was once more in silence save for the heating ducts gently blowing hot air from the upper ceiling. He got a text and squinted down to his screen.

5 minutes. Close to Shoreditch
Jay
Good. Tell me when u done
H

He padded into the bedroom with his gun raised, pulled at the wardrobe door and pointed the pistol. All he could see was his own reflection on the inside of the door. He rubbed his jaw and breathed out calmly. The hissing of the heating vent seemed to be getting louder as his heart pounded in his head.

He entered the spare bedroom and hit the light, but it was broken. He switched on his phone light and held his gun forward.

Simon looked up as a couple jumped on the bus. The guy was vaping as the door closed and the bus conductor banged on his cubicle and shouted at him to stop. He placed it back in his pocket and the couple giggled as they sat at the back. The man in the hoodie was still there. Hood still down. As Simon's stop came, he reached to the bell and pulled himself up with his good arm to stand.

Hunter stepped back up to the treadmill and placed his phone on its shelf. His pistol in the cubby hole. When he lifted his hand up, he noticed his fingers were red. He rubbed his fingers together and saw that they were powdery with fine red crystals. He noticed that the cubby was covered in the stuff. Like red sandy dust. He looked up to the ceiling and rubbed his hands down his shirt making red finger marks down his white T-shirt as he started the treadmill.

As Simon stepped off the bus, he noticed the guy in the hoodie had got off too.

He began to panic and walk briskly towards Arnold Circus. He stopped at a corner and looked back, but the man was gone. Simon could feel the sweat tingling on his neck.

He was almost running as he turned into Old Nichol Street. He approached the entrance to his building. He reached into his pocket and fumbled for his keys. He thrust his hand into his inner pocket and pulled them out but they fell onto the pavement. He switched on his phone torch and bent down. The steps approached.

Snipe's Special Drink

The noise of the party became muffled as Tom closed the pantry door. He stood in front of the other boys to explain the plan. 'So, this is what we'll do. Me, Righty and Sticks'll distract him. Lefty and Curly can put it in his tankard. I'll take care of the rest afterwards. Put some gin in his beer while you're at it, lads. A lot. We need to make sure he conks out good and proper. I've got something special to add too.'

Tom showed them the jute package.

'You're going to put paint chemical in his beer?' Curly said.

'That's right, Curly. Paint chemical.'

They all nodded to each other.

Curly hid the laxative tin under his jacket, walked round the edge of the warehouse and the others casually walked through the party into the middle of the room. They briefly danced on the crowded floor and walked to the bar.

With his head bowed, Tom walked straight up to Arthur Snipe. Snipe slowly put his tankard down and looked at him suspiciously.

Then Tom held out his hand.

At first Snipe frowned, his forehead crinkling like the top of a pasty. Tom bowed his head lower. Then Snipe succumbed and held his hand out and gripped Tom's tiny hand.

'I see you've come to your senses. That's more like it. Now get me a refill. There's a good lad. Go on, son.'

Snipe drained his tankard and passed it to Tom.

'And make it snappy,' Snipe added.

Tom carried the cup over to the front of the bar and was met by Curly who pointed down below to the bar behind him. Tom could just see the top of Lefty's head as Curly lowered the tankard.

Just then Theodore Hush appeared.

'Mr Hush. Can I get you anything? Anything at all that would wet your whistle. I am 'aving such a lovely time at this party you know,' Tom said.

Hush looked confused and moved to where Curly had been, who was now crouching down behind the bar next to Lefty.

''Ere, Mr Hush, look at her over there, she is lovely isn't she? The one there without her bodice. Bending over the chair with the other lady. Look!'

Hush started to crane his neck to try to see.

Tom nodded back to Curly, and Lefty added the gin and the Brooklax into the tankard.

'Where do you mean, Tom? You're talking ballocks, son, I can't see her.'

'There. No there,' Tom pointed over in two directions.

Tom handed back the 'frey's and the boys unpicked the sticky material and dissolved it in the drink, Lefty stirring with his stump.

Curly lifted the tankard up and passed it to Tom.

'Enjoy the party, Mr Hush,' he whispered under his breath.

Hush narrowed his eyes at Tom, turned to try to see the ladies once more and then gave up, turning back to the bar.

Tom brought the drink over, and Snipe took a long mouthful, ignoring him completely. He looked into the cup, licked his teeth and then drank back another gulp, resuming the conversation with the person standing next to him.

That night, Tom became Snipe's private waiter, going back and forth on several occasions. After all, he did want to please Mr Snipe as much as he possibly could.

Soon the party had taken over both floors of the warehouse. Tom mingled amongst the other guests trying to keep an eye on Snipe from a distance and was surprised the man was still standing. The other lads could be seen enjoying themselves like all the others, dancing, drinking and laughing. He took one last look for Snipe and could see him talking to a lady who was yawning a lot. He took this chance to make his move.

He walked up the people-strewn stairs towards Snipe's office. A tall blonde lady looped her scarf around Tom's neck and blew him a kiss, Tom feigned a laugh, wriggled free and pressed on up the stairs. Then one of the Chinese fellas grabbed him by the arm and started dancing, his face sweating. Tom played along for a while as he looked down at the party and then up to the office. He finally broke away and stepped up to the landing. He looked back, edged along the corridor wall and slipped into the office, carefully closing the door behind him.

Inside was so silent Tom could hear his own heart beating. The first thing he saw was a desk and chair near a back window. Then he saw the gold watch sitting on top of a pile of papers. He reached over and took it in his hand, remembering its weight. Its significance.

Then he saw something that made his stomach turn to ice. Snipe's yellow waistcoat was on the back of the chair. The sound of someone singing and loudly urinating was coming from the next-door privy.

Tom ducked and lay flat under the desk, his heart beating out of his mouth. He was still holding the watch.

Tom could see Snipe's legs scraping along the floor and his body moving from side to side like a top-heavy ship in a storm. He stopped at the desk. There was a short silence followed by gurgling words of some kind.

'I'm 'Enery the eight... the... watch... Mother?'

Snipe let out a laugh and then collapsed to the floor. Papers from the desk flying into the air and then flopping down on top of him.

His face was now squashed into the floor just in front of Tom. He could feel his foul breath rasping onto him as he started to snore.

Tom edged out from under the desk. Looking at the watch one last time, he turned it over in his hand and slipped it into the pocket of Snipe's waistcoat.

The party below was getting ever more raucous. Everything blended together in one slow-moving mass of sound, light and colour. Petticoats waved, top hats bowed, legs gyrated and bottles smashed. Food was thrown across the room and everything crashed together, lines of shapes converging, splicing, intersecting diagonals. Faces became cubes, eyes merging with lips and skin, white light, heat and sweat. The piano notes echoed and bounced out of the warehouse window as the storm banged in the distance. The rain began to hiss down on the warehouse roof.

The blue doors of the 'frey's laboratory slammed shut. Tom woke.

He raised his head, held his stomach and limped over to the back of the building. The clock on the factory wall said it was one minute past two. Light flashed behind the dark shapes of horses eating their feed. Tom used one of the horses to steady himself as he vomited, foamy beer splashing all over his shoes.

'Sorry, horse,' he said as he patted her.

He wiped his mouth and looked for some water. All the guests had left. Food and empty beer bottles were strewn across the battlefield of the warehouse floor. A bodice was hanging from the metal steps like a giant snake skin. Shoes and other items of clothing were spread across the scene. A tobacco pipe was stuck into a pie on top of the piano. He could hear Arthur Snipe's loud snoring still coming from upstairs.

He returned to the back warehouse and bent down to drink some water from the outside tap. As he did so, he noticed the blue doors to the secret room were jammed shut but instead of the latch being locked from the outside, it was twisted in. He spotted a keg jemmy leaning up against the wall, and once again looked up to hear if Snipe was still snoring.

Jemmying the door open was easy enough, and he slowly entered the dark space. He held his hand up to his mouth and nose to stop himself from inhaling the burnt chemical smell and lit a match and saw his shoes crunch down on orange brick dust. The match-light showed strange shiny pipes and metal stands, small glass bottles dimly glistened in the corner. His match burnt out so he lit another and held it to the opposite side of the room.

Upstairs in Snipe's office, wings of light flashed out of the slits of the closed curtains. Snipe was awoken by a voice downstairs. He noticed he was lying under his desk. As he carefully sat up, he looked down at his white trousers that were covered in black liquified faeces. Standing, he pulled on his waistcoat, held his pounding head and stumbled over to the sink. He bent over to drink as much water as he could.

Then a loud bubbling emanated from his belly and he ran to the office privy, pulling his trousers down and arriving just in time to release an explosion of foul black excrement into the privy water. The combined weight of the man and the power of the evacuation caused the porcelain to crack, and as he let out a violent trumpet of flatulence, the privy collapsed and a flood of dark water filled the entire office and cascaded down the stairs into the factory.

In the laboratory images flickered low down to Tom's right as his eyes adjusted to the darkness.

'There you are,'

He shook Curly's shoulder but he just fell forward. His face like white putty.

All the boys were sitting in a line against the wall. Sleeping faces of white stone.

'Curly? Sticks? Lads, what happened? What've you done, you bloody idiots? My God almighty, what has happened?'

Tom ran out of the room sobbing gently at first, the sobs giving way to a wail, his screams echoing around the whole warehouse. He dropped to his knees and felt the book of prayer through the lump in his jacket pocket.

At the other end of the warehouse, Arthur Snipe tumbled down the stairs and ran to where the noise was coming from.

He looked into the laboratory and recoiled back out again accidentally kicking a discarded bottle and tripping backwards to the floor.

Standing, again he looked in briefly at the dead boys and rubbed his face to think then stopped. He jerked his head around.

'To-om. Where are you, Tom?' he called, almost as if he were singing.

He picked through the building as quietly as he could, his boots crunching on broken glass. The thunder rolled above like barrels smashing down a flight of stairs.

He moved into the entrance hall, twisting his head up the stairs.

'This was an accident, I swear it. Wasn't me. They're not very clever, Tom. Not like you. They wasn't thinking. Someone must've knocked the door last night.'

He rolled a beer keg out of the way and darted his eyes from left to right.

Then he heard a tapping at the back of the building. He ran over and followed the sound. He knew exactly what it was.

Snipe turned to the courtyard and saw him. He stared at the boy with eyes of pity but also veiled aggression. Primed.

'We can talk about this, Tom. I trust you, mate. I know you won't tell no one. You're part of the family.'

'You've got nothing to offer me, Mr Snipe, and nothing left to take.'

He lifted Lady above his head, fixing Snipe's gaze.

Snipe's eyes widened like a rabid dog.

The wind blew through the warehouse. The crumpled page stirred, lifted, and floated out of the back doors.

Tom turned and ran out into the courtyard and jumped over the road towards St Leonards. As he turned left, away from the Old Nichol, he could sense Snipe a few paces behind him.

Running up Hackney Road past Ye Old Axe, Tom felt the rain beginning to come down in hard darts, the thunder smashing into the trees above.

Snipe, breathing heavily, was smiling with teeth bared as he began to catch up. Tom slowed down and looked around. He jumped into Yorkton Street and found a narrow space behind a public house. He squeezed behind some old barrels and watched the street. His breathing poured condensation out of his mouth and around him as he tried to control his shaking body.

The page drifted up the road towards Bethnal Green.

As Snipe slowed to assess the chase, he doubled over to catch his breath, the rain shiny on his bald head. He walked slowly, keenly observing any sound or movement.

Tom slowly stepped out into the street and squinted through the rain to see if he could spot Snipe on Hackney Road. Satisfied all was clear, he edged like a crab with his back to the trees by the city farm. Turning around one last time, he made his way up Goldsmith's Row, the sound of pigs and horses to his left through the violent thunder. The rain now seemed to be running down the road like a river.

As he turned, a smiling Snipe appeared, just a few paces ahead of him, beckoning with his hand to Tom.

'Give it to me and nothing will happen.'

Tom moved a few steps closer to Snipe and stopped, jerking to his left. Snipe matched his movement and shifted to block him like a dog with a squirrel. Tom tried to run to his right but Snipe was too fast and caught him. Tom struggled and almost broke free. Snipe held him around his neck from behind. He spoke into Tom's ear.

'Now, that wasn't so bad, was it?'

Snipe held Tom by the throat, licked his lips and with a flex of his arm gripped Lady's handle tight. He lifted her higher.

Fluttering past Tom, the page landed wetly on Snipe's face. He pealed the page away and squinted down at it. It stirred and blew away down Goldsmith's Row.

Tom let out a screeching whistle through his fingers and the thunder seemed to grow louder as a rhythmic thudding approached. The gate to the city farm exploded, horses rearing up and over Snipe, hooves smashing down into his flabby face with a sideways spray of rain and blood. Lady hit the ground and went skimming over the soaked road to Tom, who bent down to take it and ran up Goldsmith's Row.

Arthur Snipe ran after Tom like a wild animal, bloody rain running through his teeth and down his mouth.

The page flew up ahead of Tom and tumbled up to the gasometer.

The tradesmans' shops flew past Tom. He turned right at the pub onto Andrews Road, the street became uneven and he bounced down the hill past the warehouse.

He reached the gasometer and took out his goggles and vulcanised gloves from his bag.

Before donning his goggles, Tom caught sight of something out of place through the downpour. It was a man in night clothes at the base of the steel structure. He was smiling to Tom and holding something to his chest, one hand was bandaged. The man nodded calmly at him and gestured up to the gasometer.

The light of the storm-flashes picked out the vertical steel lines on the structure. Round bolts patterned the girders upwards. It looked like a tunnel tipped on its side; the base reflected, descending into the black water, the top reaching up to the rain-soaked sky. He could just see the dark shape of the object lodged between the girders, high up, just where he'd left it. He began to climb the frame, carefully carrying Lady up with him. Simon just looked up at Tom through the rain as the boy ascended the metal frame.

Below, Arthur Snipe stopped and smiled to himself, his eyes following Tom climbing higher.

Sparks of lightning were now shooting over the gasometer, travelling down to the top of the structure, horizontal zigzags of light smashing into either side of its metal frame, dancing in all directions.

Snipe jumped up the vertical girder like a gorilla in white trousers. Each step got him closer as Tom tried to move his short legs as quickly as he could.

As Tom pulled himself up to the second girder, he edged around the circumference to reach the dark object lodged in the steel criss-cross hole.

Lightning seemed to be moving all around the gasometer now, the odd spark hitting the metal frame with fizzy dots cascading out and falling down. A huge lightning bolt came smashing down and electrified the whole fence that enclosed the gasometer, the charge moving towards the canal and fizzing into the water.

Tom pulled on the slippery object but it wouldn't move as it was too tightly jammed in the girder. He had to lift it high above his head to dislodge it. He could see Arthur Snipe to the side of his eye approaching quickly.

The object came loose and Tom almost dropped it.

He managed to hook it over the wrist of his left hand as he carried Lady with his right.

Snipe saw his chance and moved to try to take Lady from him, but Tom anticipated the move and pulled it away just in time. Snipe slipped. He almost fell and swung on one arm like an ape as Tom moved higher, the thunder smashing down on them.

'Do you like games, Mr Snipe? I do,' Tom shouted above the din of the storm as he climbed higher.

He started to count.

'This is *my* game. Are you enjoying it?'

He counted again.

Snipe grabbed up at Tom's leg and pulled as hard as he could but his rain-soaked shoe slipped out of his hand as Tom lurched away once more.

As Snipe was getting in closer, Tom held Lady up in the air to him with his right hand.

Tom counted one last time.

With his left hand, Tom flicked open the silky object. The umbrella covered his whole head and shoulders, crackles of lightning undulated over its surface in spidery networks. Its dark blue mass bellowing in the strong wind as the white light came powering down.

He closed his eyes, reached over to Snipe and let go of Lady.

All became white.

In it Snipe saw the boys in the factory then the dog's eyes pleading. Begging as Lady struck again and again. Then to Tom. Sitting in the dock. His pleading eyes. The brothel, Snipe's profits piling high. His new gang assembled. They coshed gentlemen for their purses, robbing, murdering, maiming. Now to the old road where Snipe grew up and stole apples and pies, knocking over barrows as he disappeared into crowds. He felt the dimple in the bed where his mother once laid. Snipe wept as they pulled her hands away from his through the steel prison bars. Back at home, his father struck him and blood trickled down his mouth. Then the bell rang as he attended church school. Arthur Snipe was in his nappies, squealing in his crib. Legs wiggling in the air. Helpless. Alone. Invisible.

A blue seam of phosphorus fire shot down Lady's entire length and travelled back up Snipe's arm to his pocket watch at his chest. For a few seconds, all you could see was a glowing, fiery T-shape at the top of the gasometer. Snipe's eyes bulged from either the realisation of what had happened, or with the sheer power of the electricity coursing through his shaking body. Soon his whole face was on fire and his skin melted and dripped over his shoulders. One eyeball popped like a burst egg, his body exploding into flames, ash and sparks rising, before falling like a sizzling hog into a boat moving slowly up the canal.

The canal boat driver jumped out of his cabin, looked back at the smouldering pile of flesh and looked up to Tom as his boat passed.

Harry Simpson was no longer in the coal business. He was in the rubbish game now.

E quisquilia Lux et vis — From rubbish, light and power. Tom thought.

The soaked page flapped against the base of the gasometer.

On it was an illustration of a young boy entirely covered by a large umbrella, as a violent lightning storm raged overhead.

An elderly gentleman relates that in his youth he was struck by lightning that fell upon a silk umbrella which he held open. He saw himself enveloped in a vortex of flame, and believed himself saved by Divine protection.

Tom closed the steaming umbrella and slowly climbed down from the gasometer, bent down and unpeeled the page from the girder.

Simon Beaver, in soaked dressing gown slowly passed the book over to Tom who opened it, carefully smoothed the page back inside and placed it into his shoulder bag next to his other favourite book. It was simply called *Chelsea in Pictures*. On the cover was a painting of Tite Street on a rusty autumn afternoon. In the background, an elegant woman sat on a cycle, her long hair floating in the wind, a beauty mark on her right cheek.

Next to the gasometer, four small figures could be seen. All their body-shapes unclear in the dark seemed to flicker, appear and disappear through the remaining rain and lightning flashes. By their side, a one-eyed dog sat patiently upright.

One of the boys blankly spoke. His rasping voice like metal scraping against metal.

'The punishment has matched the crime.'

The punishment has matched the crime, all four boys repeated.

Then one of the boys sang the next line as if in church.

'The sins have been cleansed by the light.'

The sins have been cleansed by the light, the boys repeated, with choral harmonies.

They looked to Tom once more, turned and followed him back towards Shoreditch.

Theodore Hush

Water drops clanked into steel buckets dotted across the floor of the shop. Theodore Hush wrenched up the door blind looking outside to the left and right, poking his lamp against the window. He pulled the blind back down. A blanket had been placed against the door's base and Hush kicked it closer into the gap before walking to the counter. He shook his head and pulled the lever at the counter.

At the back of the shop, the smell was more damp than usual and you could still hear the last taps of rainfall in the back alley. Hush whistled to himself as he shuffled to the pantry area and reached up for the kettle on the hook.

Then he heard it again and stopped — it was singing. A choir of some sort.

Strange that. You wouldn't be able to hear St Leonards all the way down here and, anyway, what were they doing at this hour?

He stopped moving and squinted in the low light, his mouth making a round shape as he strained his head forward to listen.

'Good evening, Mr Hush.'

'Fuuuuck, Tom! You frightened the living wits out of me.'

'We've come to say hello.'

'What the 'ell you on about? Anyway, I thought you was at the party.'

'The party is over, Mr Hush. They're gone. They've all gone. And, anyway, I've been thinking...'

'Oh, don't do that, son, you might give yourself a headache,' he said laughing.

'No, I think you're wrong about that, Mr Hush. Thinking is good. Thinking helps you plan.'

'What the hell you on about, Tom? How did you get in here anyway? You look a bit pale, son, you alright? You look different.'

'I've never felt better, Mr Hush.'

Tom's tone then changed to a voice of pretend fear.

'Mr Snipe sent me to get something. He was ever so angry when he asked me.'

'*Angry* you say?'

'Yes. He said he already asked you.'

'Oh, you should have said, Tom. What is it?'

'A clock. He wants it for the office.'

'What's he want with a clock? It's the middle of the bloody night.'

'You know how he is with the trinkets, Mr Hush.'

'Typical. Alright, which one? Hurry up, it's late, Tom.'

Yawning, Hush reached over to the lever to release the curtain and faced Tom as he spoke.

'You know, I think I do remember him saying something about a clock come to think of it. Mr Snipe has his ways as you know and it's never a good idea to...'

As the curtain swished across, on the raised platform in front of the wall of clocks stood Curly, Sticks, Lefty and Righty. They were all smiling.

'What the fuckin hell...'

Hush jumped back but Tom pushed him up on the platform with the boys. Sticks stood over him and pulled his right arm wide as Tom and Curly pulled his left arm in the other direction.

'What is this? What you lot doin' here?'

Hush tried to struggle free so Lefty kicked him in his ballocks and Curly pulled his head back again. Then Tom spoke.

'Now, lads, what did I say about voltage, remember?'

'It is estimated that 100–125 volts can cause death but it is thought that supplies as low as 42 can cause harm and can be fatal in certain circumstances.'

'Very good, boys. Now, is gold an efficient conductor?'

They all answered together like bored schoolchildren.

'Gold is a conductor of electricity like other metals. The delocalized electrons, present in the free space surrounding the gold atoms, act as free charge carriers which help in the conduction of electricity when a voltage source is applied.'

'Well, it's lucky that we happen to have an awful lot of the material... right here!'

Tom gestured with both hands raised to the wall of clocks, like a magician at the playhouse.

He then retrieved the blackened handle of Lady from his pocket, the woman's face was mangled and distorted, the hair melted into a round blob of hardened silver. Tom threw it into the air and caught it, holding it right up to Hush.

'It's not as conductive as silver but we'll just have to manage, eh?'

Hush began to whimper and scream. His legs began to tremble.

'What have you done with him? Tom. Tom, don't you dare... don't do this. I'm begging you, mate.'

All the boys pushed Hush back against the clocks. Lefty placed his good hand up into one of the carriage clocks then stuck his stump into Hush's left ear to which Tom nodded. Righty then placed his hand on another clock and did the same with Hush's right ear, completing the circuit. Hush tried to move and wriggle out of the way. Curly punched him in the stomach and Sticks held him in place. Hush started to urinate, a dark patch growing in his crotch.

'Oh dear, careful, Mr Hush, there's already an awful lot of water in the shop after the storm,' Tom said, tutting through his teeth and waving his finger.

'So, what's it to be, lads? A nice slow 40 volts first and then we could *play it by ear.'*

All the boys laughed, as a low hum filled the room.

Theodore Hush's head started to shake as he began to scream. His hair moved in all directions and his eyeballs grew wilder as the volts increased. Sparks began flying from his ears down to the water on the shop's floor as he convulsed more violently. Soon the air was filled with a burning meat smell combined with singed wool.

The water below started to fizz gently; the wall of clocks began to illuminate with blue-white lines that traced each horological feature like a million glowing, marching ants. As Hush's face started to melt, the clocks also began to drip, until the floor was a mass of steaming water and liquid gold.

Eventually, all that remained poking up from the watery floor were blackened clock parts like metal skeletons.

Lefty and Righty removed their arms from what remained of Hush's ears. Hush was now stuck vertically, a burnt carcass cooked into the grill of clocks behind him. Half his mouth was melted, exposing his teeth in a forced grin.

The boys stepped down, heads lowered.

Curly began.

'The punishment has matched the crime.'

The punishment has matched the crime, all four boys repeated.

Righty sang the next line.

'The sins have been cleansed by the light.'

The sins have been cleansed by the light, all four boys sang in unison.

Before stepping out of the shop with the other boys, Tom looked down to the burnt umbrella in his hand and placed it back up on the wall, just where he had first seen it. They filed through Boundary Passage.

The Light

Time moved forward. Years fell away. Wars and revolutions came and went. Peace, war and revolution began again. Leaves floated down like giant insects before settling onto the circle of benches, a jagged carpet of red and ochre filling the park.

Tom Baxter opened his eyes.

He looked down and noticed his whole body was invisible. He thought it curious that this fact wasn't alarming. In fact, he felt quite relaxed about it.

But how could he see if his eyes were invisible? How could he feel his arms if they weren't there either? He pondered upon that philosophical question for a few minutes and then looked up. He seemed to be lying on a bench in what looked like a small round park. The night sky was a slate grey. At least that was something familiar. The buildings around the park were strange and modern, like the ones Vanessa had showed him.

The first sound that he noticed was a distant humming. Like a machine or swarm of giant bees. It wasn't near, but seemed to be all around him.

He sat up and instinctively patted where his arms would be, and sure enough loose earth and red dust particles briefly appeared and then blew away on the wind. His eyes followed the dust and then he looked down again. His whole body had returned. His arms legs and feet. He was even wearing his familiar brown woollen jacket. His hat was on his head.

Then he saw a movement just beyond the bandstand. On another bench, right opposite, Curly sat up looking bewildered.

'Oi, Curly!'

'Oh, hello, Tom. What's goin' on?'

'Search me. Just got here.'

'Curly, you can see me.'

'Course I can, I'm talkin' to you, aren't I?'

'Look at yourself.'

Curly looked down at his own arms and legs.

'Bloody 'ell. So, *we* can see each other but we can't see *ourselves.*'

'Not for long. It doesn't last.'

'Ladies!'

Over to the right, Sticks was waving with his gangly arms above his head from another park bench.

Righty and Lefty sauntered into the middle of the park.

'Boys,' they just said, as if they'd just returned after going for a quick piss behind a tree. In fact, if ghosts did piss this might well have been the case.

They all grouped together around Tom.

'Your eyes look strange, Curly.'

'So do yours, Tom.'

'Righty, Lefty, show me your eyes. Sticks?'

'Looks like we're all the same. Black as night,' Tom said.

'Tom, I don't like this. I'm scared. What's happened to us?'

Tom held Curly's shoulders and looked into his black eyes the best he could without looking scared himself.

'Something has happened, yes. Quite what, I don't know. But we need to find out, Curly.'

'Are we... you know?' Sticks asked.

'Yes. I think we're in Shoreditch,' Curly said, looking around.

'No, Curly, you idiot. Are we ghosts?' Lefty said.

'It... it seems we are, Lefty,' Tom said

'But I don't want to be a ghost. How did we die? What happened to us?' Curly said.

Tom looked to the floor.

'Well, we can't stay here all night. Let's head back to the factory at least,' Righty said.

'Yes, you're right, let's get out of here,' Tom agreed.

A rustling in the leaves came from below. All the boys looked down. The one-eyed dog, his head cocked to one side was pawing the ground.

Tom bent down and scratched the dog's ear.

'Hello, boy. You found your way here too. What we goin' to call ya now you're part of the gang?'

'What about Merrychance?' Sticks said.

'Well, *Merrychance*. What do we do now?' Tom asked.

The dog just lifted his paw up.

'You're right. Let's get out of this park for starters.'

They all followed Tom in single file, each boy looking around and pointing as they chatted away.

They stopped when they emerged onto Shoreditch High Street. In the reflections of their black eyes, the lights danced and flashed. Bright lamps of many colours were on metal posts. Lights were shining in windows. Green, blue, yellow and red. Some spelt out words, some were just strips at odd angles, surrounding doorways, covering windows. Along the wet street, the lamps were reflected, doubling their height in a shimmering sea of purple and green.

The boys turned as a steam engine whistle burst into the street. A white horseless coach with blue lamps flashing appeared, its wheels spraying water up to the boys. On the side of the coach was written the word P-O-L-I-C-E. A gang of Peelers came out of its back and marched down the street.

Taverns full of people drinking and laughing were everywhere. Music too. Giant red double-height omnibus, again without horses, splashed along the streets letting passengers upon them as more alighted from the side.

Small horseless coaches of many colours with two lights like eyes raced up and down the streets as if powered by magic.

The light had won. There was electricity for all. From dust, light and life.

The Beginning

Glowing veins of electrons carve through ionised channels.

A negative charge travels down to the ground at great speed, its positively charged twin reaching up to meet it. The sky cracks apart like the lines on a vertical ice pond, as if opening a void between this world and the next.

Black fabric. A wooden pew in the front row. The ceremony was about to begin. The congregation filed in quietly. Respectfully.

A woman could be seen sitting upright in the front row. Her hand gripped a box of tissues in her lap.

The boy's leg shook under the black gown. He stood nervously and walked up to the wooden podium.

With tears in her eyes, the woman cheered and took photos with her phone held high as the audience clapped.

A man watched from the back. Grey hair. A slight stoop. He could feel the little orange book weighing his jacket pocket down. By his side a tall Asian woman cheered, a wedding ring on her hand.

As the boy lifted his diploma, he caught the man's eye and they smiled to each other across the crowded university auditorium.

In South West London the coach cut through the morning fog to Westminster and back on to Chelsea embankment. The coachman pulled the reins up and his horses stopped as a line of coaches crossed Albert Bridge.

As he waited, he noticed an African man with red shoes leaning down onto the embankment wall. His jacket collar pulled up against the cold. He seemed to be in a kind of rapture. Lost in the moment as he looked south along the Thames to Battersea and beyond.

In a London park, white confetti blossom floated across clear sky like spring snow.

Snow already fallen, covered the park in white crescent patches underneath warm tree shade.

A faded page zigzagged gently down onto a park bench and fluttered next to a pram.

Thousands of miles away, forked lightning flashed down, its rhizomes shooting in different directions, arriving at multiple destinations in one split second.

High up in the cloudless blue, the Lockheed scanned the sky from Western Europe all the way across to the Eastern Seaboard. Inside the plane's white cabin, a young Meteorologist, nervous on his maiden flight, inputted data into the chunky keyboard. High altitude sunlight made the blue birthmark on his pale cheek stand out.

He never really knew how he fell into this strange profession. He just seemed to have a good feel for it. If there was a storm to be found, he would find it.

As the plane slowly turned, blinding sun entered the cabin, the Meteorologist pulled his cap lower and watched the storm icon edge across the screen.

His boss leaned over his shoulder. As she passed him a coffee in a paper cup, her green eyes smiled, her beauty mark rising on her frown. Her auburn hair red at the edges against the bright blue sky.

Acknowledgements

I'm Henery The Eighth I am by Fred Murray and R. P. Weston (1910)

Oh! Mr Porter by George Le Brunn (1892)

Thunder and Lightning by W.D. de Fonvielle (1875)

London Fictions (an article on A Child of the Jago by Sarah Wise, Five Leaves, 2013)

A Child of the Jago by Arthur Morison (1896)

Cover photography by Christopher Campbell and Hermann Wittekopf

This book is dedicated to Nooshi, Danny, Alex, Pashmak and, of course, Hackney.

FICTION

Put simply, we publish great stories. Whether it's literary or popular, a gentle tale or a pulsating thriller, the connecting theme in all Roundfire fiction titles is that once you pick them up you won't want to put them down.
If you have enjoyed this book, why not tell other readers by posting a review on your preferred book site.

Recent bestsellers from Roundfire are:

The Bookseller's Sonnets
Andi Rosenthal
The Bookseller's Sonnets intertwines three love stories
with a tale of religious identity and mystery spanning
five hundred years and three countries.
Paperback: 978-1-84694-342-3 ebook: 978-184694-626-4

Birds of the Nile
An Egyptian Adventure
N.E. David
Ex-diplomat Michael Blake wanted a quiet birding trip
up the Nile – he wasn't expecting a revolution.
Paperback: 978-1-78279-158-4 ebook: 978-1-78279-157-7

Blood Profit$
The Lithium Conspiracy
J. Victor Tomaszek, James N. Patrick, Sr.
The blood of the many for the profits of the few... *Blood Profit$*
will take you into the cigar-smoke-filled room where American
policy and laws are really made.
Paperback: 978-1-78279-483-7 ebook: 978-1-78279-277-2

The Burden
A Family Saga
N.E. David
Frank will do anything to keep his mother and father
apart. But he's carrying baggage – and it might
just weigh him down ...
Paperback: 978-1-78279-936-8 ebook: 978-1-78279-937-5

The Cause
Roderick Vincent
The second American Revolution will be a
fire lit from an internal spark.
Paperback: 978-1-78279-763-0 ebook: 978-1-78279-762-3

Don't Drink and Fly
The Story of Bernice O'Hanlon: Part One
Cathie Devitt
Bernice is a witch living in Glasgow. She loses her way
in her life and wanders off the beaten track looking for the
garden of enlightenment.
Paperback: 978-1-78279-016-7 ebook: 978-1-78279-015-0

Gag
Melissa Unger
One rainy afternoon in a Brooklyn diner, Peter Howland
punctures an egg with his fork. Repulsed, Peter pushes
the plate away and never eats again.
Paperback: 978-1-78279-564-3 ebook: 978-1-78279-563-6

The Master Yeshua
The Undiscovered Gospel of Joseph
Joyce Luck
Jesus is not who you think he is. The year is 75 CE. Joseph
ben Jude is frail and ailing, but he has a prophecy to fulfil ...
Paperback: 978-1-78279-974-0 ebook: 978-1-78279-975-7

On the Far Side, There's a Boy
Paula Coston

Martine Haslett, a thirty-something 1980s woman, plays hard on the fringes of the London drag club scene until one night which prompts her to sign up to a charity. She writes to a young Sri Lankan boy, with consequences far and long.
Paperback: 978-1-78279-574-2 ebook: 978-1-78279-573-5

Tuareg
Alberto Vazquez-Figueroa

With over 5 million copies sold worldwide, *Tuareg* is a classic adventure story from best-selling author Alberto Vazquez-Figueroa, about honour, revenge and a clash of cultures.
Paperback: 978-1-84694-192-4

Readers of ebooks can buy or view any of these bestsellers by clicking on the live link in the title. Most titles are published in paperback and as an ebook. Paperbacks are available in traditional bookshops. Both print and ebook formats are available online.

Find more titles and sign up to our readers' newsletter at www.collectiveinkbooks.com/fiction